The Mysterious Shootings at

THE ROUTE 66 RANCH HOTEL

By

N.C.L. SARNO

The Mysterious Shootings at The Route 66
Ranch Hotel
Copyright © 2023 N.C.L. Sarno

The Mysterious Shootings at The Route 66
Ranch Hotel is a work of fiction. Names,
characters, places, and incidents either are the
product of the author's imagination or are used
fictitiously. Any resemblance to actual persons,
living or dead, organizations, events or locales is
entirely coincidental.

Cover by N.C.L. Sarno

KDP ISBN: 9798877171626

Dedicated to La Posada,

the crown jewel of Arizona Route 66 historic hotels,

to Mary Colter for envisioning this masterpiece,

and to all the people who painstakingly refurbished this treasure to its former glory.

CONTENTS

Chapter One

"Sunset!" Eve called out towards the setting sun. She was glad there were not yet guests at her rural hotel who might mistake her shout as a bizarrely exuberant announcement of the time of day. She wasn't a crazy person; she was merely calling out for her dog named Sunset.

Shortly after she had named Sunset almost two months earlier, she had realized that she had plagued her poor dog with a noun as a name. She always felt sorry for people who had to deal with the confusion that arises from having a noun as a first name. *Turn the page, Page. Bill, did you pay that bill? You must have hope, Hope. Cliff, don't fall off the –*

Eve knew the indignities herself when she was a child in school. At first, she only suffered as the end of the year neared when the children were once again reminded to call her "Christmas" Eve and "New Year's" Eve. Then, the children learned the term eavesdropping and developed a line of ill-crafted jokes about Eve's dropping this and Eve's dropping that. She spent a few years of her childhood making sure to never drop anything in front of her classmates. As she got older, she tried to explain to the kids that 'eaves' was spelled differently than 'Eve's' so their joke didn't make sense. They didn't care. After all, Matt was spelled differently than the mat that you wiped your feet on, and they didn't care about that.

She had thought her only alternative was to start going by her full name, Genevieve, but that seemed like it might be a lateral move in the high-stakes world of grammar school teasing. *But perhaps that is a thing of the past,* Eve mused. Nowadays people are naming their children all sorts of unconventional names. Maybe the elementary schools are now so full of noun names that the kids don't single them out anymore. After all, how could an Asteroid possibly make fun of a Banjo?

And Sunset was now Sunset; there was no going back. He knew his name as he proved by running back towards Eve instead of getting into some dusky mischief. She was overjoyed at the gradual, yet surprisingly fast, transition Sunset had made from being a wild young dog, scared of humans, to the attentive loving companion he now was.

They walked into the front door of the hotel. Decades ago, the hotel had been known as The Arizona Sunset Ranch Hotel, which was one of the reasons Eve had chosen the name Sunset for her dog. The secluded hotel would soon be opening for its second act as The Route 66 Ranch Hotel.

She had just returned from buying the last horse for her trail riding business at the hotel. Tempest, a striking red and white American Paint with a white mane and a black tail, was horse number seven. She had been the favorite mount of Eve's horse wrangler, Wes, at his previous job at Darlin' Darla's Dude Ranch outside of Tucson.

Darla had called and offered to sell the prized mare to Eve at a good price since she had a soft spot for Wes. But Darla insisted Wes come down to pick Tempest up himself so that Darla could "see his cute butt again."

Darla explained to Eve that she could say that now since Wes wasn't her employee any longer. Eve had been fascinated by Darlin' Darla's loud-living personality during their phone conversations and wanted to meet her in person, so she accompanied Wes for the long trip. Not only had the excursion offered a very informative tour of the dude ranch which helped Eve gather information for her own upcoming business venture, but meeting Darla had also indeed been a hoot (a term Eve picked up from Darla herself). After visiting southern Arizona in the brutal heat of the summer, she understood why Wes had only worked there in the winters and relocated to a full-time job in the high elevation of the northern part of the state. Eve thought that Tempest may also appreciate the climate of her new home.

Tempest had joined the new horse family at The Route 66 Ranch Hotel that included Butterscotch, Gertie, Handsome, Maverick, Dakota, and Morning Dew. Eve was in awe of her stunning collection of horses. She had worked diligently with Wes the last few weeks to acquire good trail riding horses that were available in Northern Arizona. Her intention had not been to pick the most attractive horses, but that is what she felt had happened. Perhaps she was just feeling motherly pride, but she really thought her new horse children were the most beautiful in the world. She also loved that they were all so different, each a different breed and unique color combination. Butterscotch was a tan mustang; Gertie, a gray and white spotted Appaloosa; Handsome, a black Tennessee Walking Horse; Maverick, a dark brown American Quarter Horse; Dakota, a reddish-brown Morgan; and Morning Dew, a white and tan Spotted Saddle Horse. Admittedly a novice horse owner, Eve was also starting to realize that they each had their own distinct personality as well. She was looking forward to getting to know them all better.

Eve was tired from the six-hour drive back home and

was looking forward to sleeping in her own bed with Sunset at her feet. But before she succumbed to her exhaustion, she wanted to dive into her new reading material: her Great Aunt Genevieve's diaries. On their way back home, she and Wes had picked up the mail at the post office in their closest town of Sandmat. Eve had been overjoyed to finally receive the package from her cousin, Ruby. (Ruby and her sister, Pearl, had never been teased about their noun names. Apparently, precious jewels were exempt.)

After learning of their existence, Eve had been impatiently awaiting the delivery of the dozens of diaries. Eve had been completely unaware that her Great Aunt Genevieve, whom Eve herself was named after, had been an avid chronicler of her life. When Ruby recently unearthed the treasures that she had unknowingly inherited a few years ago, she immediately called Eve to ask if she wanted them. Ruby knew that Eve loved history, especially anything related to their great aunt.

After Genevieve's passing, Eve inherited the Arizona ranch hotel property and thrown herself into renovating the buildings that had sat vacant for the last few decades. Originally, the property had been built and owned by Genevieve's wealthy boss, Mr. Alfred Thorton. Genevieve had been Mr. Thorton's assistant, working and traveling with him for nearly her entire life. Genevieve had spent a lot of time at the Arizona ranch over the years and had often spoken of her affection for it. Eve was dedicated to finding out as much as possible about the history of the property, the ranch, and especially the hotel. The diaries were likely to answer many of Eve's questions. She couldn't wait.

Sunset and Eve curled up on one of the lobby couches in the empty hotel. She had chosen one of the diaries from the early 1970s. She skimmed through the entries, looking for references to the ranch. She had every intention of reading the diaries cover to cover eventually, but she had a very specific project she was working on right now and wanted to focus on finding any additional information about her inherited property.

She would soon be hosting a group of some of the previous hotel employees from approximately half a century ago. She planned to mine them for information about the property's history while they acted as the first guests at the newly renovated hotel. As she read the diary, she searched for information that might help guide her interviews during the Arizona Sunset Ranch Hotel reunion. She especially wanted to learn what the hotel was like when it serviced the busy traffic on Route 66 back in its heyday.

Eve had already known that the building acted as a hotel when Mr. Thorton was not in residence. When he flew in for a stay at his vacation property in Arizona (using the small airstrip on the property) the hotel staff transitioned to his personal staff, providing for Mr. Thorton and his private guests. But her new diary collection did not disappoint in teaching her something new about the workings of Mr. Thorton's hotel and vacation home. Eve read:

September 19, 1971

We are finally leaving New York tomorrow. Our long-awaited respite in Arizona has been delayed day after day due to this problematic merger. Finally, and thankfully, all of the dots are on every i and the crosses have been slashed across every t. It has been nearly a week's deferment to our original plan. Since it is the custom of the Arizona staff to vacate guests from the hotel a full week before our arrival in preparation, the hotel staff has been idle for days. I hope Walter and Constance will not be too cross with me. Not that they would ever say a word. They are such dears. I am quite looking forward to seeing their daughter, Annabelle. She is such a sweetly spirited young thing. I believe she is now seven! It seems like only yesterday that Constance had realized she was with child. How the years melt away!

Not only was Eve interested to learn that the staff always cleared the hotel a full week before Mr. Thorton's arrival, but she was overjoyed to read a reference to two of her soon to be guests: Walter Flint and his daughter, Annabelle.

Eve had been in contact with Annabelle who was looking forward to bringing her 87-year-old father back to the property that he had worked at for 42 years, the entire time the property was functioning. He started in 1956 when the hotel first opened and eventually became the property manager. Walter continued in that role for decades, even after the interstate by-pass ceased travel on this stretch of Route 66 and the hotel was forced to close and the large building was used only as a vacation residence. Walter finally retired in 1998, at which time Mr. Thorton stopped using the property altogether. Annabelle had told Eve that, after her mother's passing, her father had become depressed. She was hoping that this trip might help him to remember the good old days at the ranch.

Eve's mind was now back in the present and could not focus on the past. She had so many things to do before the arrival of her first hotel guests. She grabbed some paper and a pen and started to hurriedly scribble down the information she wanted to go over with her staff in the morning. She wanted everything to be perfect for her very first hotel guests.

Chapter Two

Eve was up early, as was her custom, and was walking along the paved ranch road that they called the driveway. As she and Sunset walked toward Historic Route 66, Eve gazed out at the spectacular show that August in Northern Arizona was putting on for her. Last summer, her first summer living in her new home of Northern Arizona, she had been surprised to find that July and August were the months of monsoons. Just as last year, the season of storms had painted the arid landscape green. The usually brown, brittle, wild grasses came to life with the rare rains. Dark but dormant clouds were scattered throughout the morning sky creating dramatic streaks of light speckling the hills and valleys with glowing spots.

As she and Sunset walked down the road, a bird joined them. The bird perched upon the top of the old ranch fence until Eve and Sunset arrived at its location. When they arrived, the bird would then fly farther down the fence, land again, and wait for them. This went on and on until the bird finally tired of the game and flew off for good. This happened on a regular basis on their walks.

7

She wondered if it was the same bird who had a particular fondness for her and Sunset, or if it was a common game enjoyed by all birds. Eve liked birds (certainly enough to spend a small fortune on bird seed, suet, and nectar every month) but she knew little about her friends of flight. She just knew she liked having them around. Being surrounded by adorable chirping birds made her feel like she was a fairy tale princess.

Suddenly, she remembered she had called an early staff meeting this morning. She looked at her watch and realized she would be late for her own meeting if she didn't hurry back right away.

"Okay, Sunset, let's race back home," she said to her canine companion.

Sunset was more than willing to accept the challenge. Eve had no hope of winning the footrace (or the foot/paw race) against her young dog, but she certainly hadn't expected to immediately start gasping like an asthmatic smoker. In her previous life, she could go for a jog without such severe effects. She needed to start exercising more. She knew that Sunset would be more than happy to turn their daily walks into daily jogs. He was already waiting on the front porch of the hotel happily wagging his tail, celebrating his victory. Eve stopped running and clutched her side as she began to walk and tried to slow her breath. She would rather be late to her own meeting than show up breathless and sweaty. The moment of feeling like a fairy tale princess had completely vanished.

***

Armed with her scribbled notes from the night before, Eve addressed her staff. At this point, they were less like staff and more like family to Eve, and most of them were actually family to each other. Her housekeeping staff were a mother and daughter pair: Loretta and Roxie. Esperanza, her cook, was married to Ramon, Eve's right-hand-man and jack-of-all-trades. Only Wes, her horse wrangler, was unrelated. But in a very short time the group had become very close.

"I know I have said it many times before, but I want to thank you all again for offering to work overtime and do whatever is needed while we embark on the beginning stages of this endeavor," Eve said to her employees that were seated on the lobby couches and chairs having their morning coffee. "I think you have all figured out by now that I don't actually know how to run a hotel." She smiled before she punctuated her comment with a "YET!"

"We'll figure it out together," Esperanza said reassuringly.

"Exactly," said Eve. "And together we'll determine the additional staff we'll need. Please, remember, I am relying on your input during these early days."

"Is the Grand Opening still next Saturday?" asked Loretta.

"Not next Saturday. We will have the previous hotel employees here then," replied Eve.

"I didn't say this Saturday, I said next Saturday," Loretta said.

"But this Saturday is next Saturday," said Ramon. "The next Saturday is this Saturday."

"What?" asked Roxie.

"The next Saturday that we will be experiencing is at the end of this week," Ramon explained. "Therefore, that day will be both 'this' coming Saturday as well as the 'next' Saturday. If you were first in a line at a store and the clerk called out 'next person' would they mean you? Or would they say 'No, not you, you are not the next person, you are the this person'?

Roxie looked perplexed while her mother, Loretta, exaggerated her wild eyeroll by also rolling her head backward as she exclaimed, "Okay, whatever! Is the grand opening the Saturday after this Saturday, like the one in two weeks or whatever?"

"Yes," said Eve with a smile as she reflected how being close like a family also meant getting annoyed with each other and bickering like a family. "Our schedule for the next two weeks is what I wanted to go over with you this morning. Our first guests, or pre-guests, the previous hotel employees, will arrive tomorrow. They will be checking in Wednesday and checking out on Monday. After they check out, we will start preparing for the Grand Opening, which will be the following Saturday — August 26 — to avoid any further confusion. We do have a few reservations for that day, but it will be mostly a day for the locals to come check us out. We'll have a barbecue and pool party similar to what we'll be doing for the Arizona Sunset Ranch Hotel employees on Friday afternoon, but on a larger scale since we'll be expecting a lot more people. Thankfully, some of Esperanza's and Ramon's family members have offered to come and help us out for the Grand Opening. Wes will be giving free, short horseback rides. And Wes's girlfriend, June, has offered to help us out with that."

"Oh, we finally get to meet the mysterious June!" said Esperanza as she winked at Wes.

"But before the Grand Opening," Eve continued, "we'll need to focus on our first challenge: throwing a great reunion for the employees of the old Arizona Sunset Ranch Hotel. I want to show them a really good time, so they don't realize that my motivation in inviting them was purely selfish."

"How many people are coming?" asked Roxie.

Eve referred to her papers. "We have nine total guests coming to stay with us. No, wait, eight. Ramon is on my list as part of the reunion group but he is already here."

Ramon had worked at the Arizona Sunset Ranch Hotel in 1976 for a few months between graduating high school and going off to college but, unfortunately, he never met Eve's great aunt Genevieve or the owner of the hotel, Mr. Thorton.

"Walter Flint and his daughter Annabelle Sheridan are coming up from the Phoenix area," Eve continued.

"Walter and his wife, Constance, ran the hotel and property for about 40 years. Their daughter, Annabelle, was born and raised here. So, that's a good reminder that these people have a much deeper connection to this property than we do. I'm very excited that they will be able to see their old home again. Walter is the eldest that will be joining us, so I had planned on giving him the downstairs accessible room so he wouldn't have to climb the stairs, but Annabelle said that her dad is still very mobile and strong and loves the exercise of stairs. And she said that she would like to have a room next to him, therefore I'm giving Walter Suite A and Annabelle the connecting room, number 3."

"We also have ranch hotel sweethearts, Tom and Julie Hayward coming from Las Vegas and they are bringing their son, Ben. Tom and Julie will be in Suite B and their son will be in Room 7. Tom and Julie met here when they were young. I think that is so sweet! Tom was the horseback riding trail guide and Julie was a housekeeper in the hotel.

"And we have L. Sterling who will be in Room 5. And he just goes by Sterling, correct?" Eve asked Ramon, who nodded his head. "I don't have that much information on him. He was the gardener, I believe."

"Gardener and the shooting range guide for the guests," said Ramon.

"We also have Millicent Buchanan coming from Payson. She will be in Room 4. She also worked here for many years during the hotel years and long after, just like Walter. She was the cook."

"And her husband was the ranch foreman," added Ramon.

"Yes, Millicent and her husband worked here for over thirty years, I believe."

"Wow. These people must be really old, right?" asked Roxie.

"Well, they can't've worked here 40 or 50 years ago

and be young," said Loretta.

"Excuse me!" said Ramon with mock offense. "Old? I have not aged at all. But I am interested to see how the others have."

"I have the years they worked here and how old they were then. I think I figured out their current ages and have them somewhere," Eve said as she shuffled through her papers. "Yes, here it is. It looks like Walter is 87, Millicent is 78, Sterling is 70, Tom is 69, Julie is 66, and Annabelle is 59."

Roxie held up her hands showing seven fingers. "That's only seven. Even with the son that's coming. It's only seven."

"Oh, I forgot Gil!" said Eve. "Do you all know Gil Dancer from Sandmat? He's the owner of the Dancer Diner and Ramon's very good friend. Which, by the way, is a friendship born out of meeting and working at this hotel together. What a magical place this is! Gil was Millicent's assistant in the kitchen when he was a young man. He will be in Room 6."

"So, they're coming the day after tomorrow, and then what?" asked Wes.

"Here is a schedule for each of you. The first page is the schedule of events that I will be giving them, and the second page is the schedule for us. I thought about organizing more events for them but then I reconsidered. They probably will just want to relax and socialize, so I have a lot of downtime in between scheduled events and history interviews."

"What's a history interview?" asked Esperanza.

"That's when I'm going to interview each old hotel employee separately and make an audio recording about their work here and any interesting stories they have. And 'Storytime' that I have planned for Friday night is when I'm going to film each of them telling their favorite story about working here. It's going to be great!"

Chapter Three

Luckily, Sunset was good with the horses since Wes often took care of him during the workday. It was a common sight to see Sunset running around the area near the stables but today Eve noticed he was frolicking with a playmate. Eve went out the back door to investigate the appearance of this new dog.

On her arrival into the stables building, after dodging the joyful leaping dogs, she found Dr. Nadar with her hand in Tempest's mouth. Naiya Nadar was the local horse veterinarian who was kind enough to take on Eve's new horses as patients even though she was already incredibly busy. She was also Sunset's house-call vet since she already came to the property for the horses. Eve was very happy with the situation. She also really liked Dr. Nadar and loved her sleek black Cleopatra haircut.

Eve waited for Dr. Nadar to finish Tempest's inspection before saying, "Good morning. I was wondering where Sunset's new companion came from."

Dr. Nadar turned around and said, "Oh, hi. Yes, that's Midas. He's with me. I hope it's okay that I brought him. I thought he and Sunset would get along, so I took a chance."

"Well, you were right. I've never seen two happier dogs."

"I know. They're adorable."

Wes walked in and said, "So, how is she doc? Perfect, right?" He reached out to Tempest and she instantly responded by leaning her head to nuzzle his hand.

Eve looked at Dr. Nadar and thrust her head toward Wes and Tempest as she said, "Those two are pretty adorable too."

Dr. Nadar nodded, laughed and said, "Yes, Wes, she is perfect." Then to Eve, "I heard you are opening soon. That's exciting."

"Yes. I hope you can make it to the grand opening on the 26th."

"But you're having guests before that correct? The hotel employees that worked here a long time ago?"

"Yes, how do you know about that?"

"Gil told me. I often eat at his diner. My talents do not extend to the culinary field. I also board his dogs when he and his wife go hunting or on vacation."

Besides her busy veterinary practice, Dr. Nadar also had a boarding facility for horses and house pets, mostly dogs. Eve had heard that the boarding facility for dogs was something to see. Apparently, it had an extensive dog park complete with an obstacle course, a sandbox, and a water feature. Thinking of it gave Eve an idea.

"Would it be possible for me to board Sunset at your place for a few days while I have the former hotel employees here? I know it's short notice, but I'm feeling a little overwhelmed and not having to worry about Sunset would take a lot off my mind. And if he could play with Midas while he's there, I'm sure he won't even notice my absence."

"Yes, that would be fine. I actually don't have any canine guests right now. Midas would love the company. I can take him with me right now if you'd like."

"Let me get his food and things together and then Sunset and I can follow you and Midas out there. I'd like to see your place. I've heard so much about it."

"Sounds great."

***

When Eve started her car, she perfunctorily made a mental note of the mileage. She always did. It was her strongest obsessive compulsion: always knowing her car's current mileage and determining the distance between every location. She knew that from the parking lot, the small town of Sandmat was a little over 27 miles away to the east, the ranch Wes's girlfriend worked on was a little under 12 miles to the west, the entrance to a bizarre little mining ghost town was 7 miles to the east, and the closest hospital was 63 miles to the west. She thought that last one was a good piece of information to know in case of any emergencies with her future guests.

She blamed her obsessive mileage checking on her ex-boyfriend in Chicago. He was a car-guy through and through and had instilled in her a monumental importance of checking her mileage and getting oil changes at or before the recommended mileage. It was now a routine that she had no control over. Therefore, as she pulled up to "The Horse and Hound Hotel" she noticed that it was exactly 15 miles (conveniently on her way to Sandmat) from her place. Eve thought it was hilarious that she now considered a location 15 miles away from her home as close. Just a couple of years ago, when she lived in Chicago, if she had to travel 15 miles, she would have considered it a road trip. Now, she thought that distance was practically next door.

"I love that we both own hotels!" Eve said as she and Dr. Nadar exited their cars and let out their dogs who acted like they had been separated for years. Eve looked around at the property. It was indeed impressive. "Except, I think yours might be nicer."

"It definitely has more amenities for the canine guests,

but your horse facilities are just as nice as mine. And as for human hotel guests — you can keep them," Dr. Nadar said as she motioned to Eve to follow her inside.

"I love the name," Eve said. "The Horse and Hound Hotel… it's reminiscent of an English pub."

Dr. Nadar stopped and turned to look at Eve. "You are the first person to get that! Or at least the first person to ever mention it. I even had the sign designed to look like an English pub hotel sign, and yet no one has ever noticed! You just made my day! I always wanted to open a English style pub and name it something silly like 'The Lazy Jogger' after myself of course, or if you had bartenders who couldn't mix drinks, call it 'The Incompetent Chemists.'"

They went to the front desk where Eve met Dr. Nadar's vet tech and office manager. She paid for Sunset's stay before getting the full tour of the facilities by Dr. Nadar, who insisted she start calling her Naiya. They were sitting on a bench in the dog park watching an overwhelmed Sunset ignore Midas. It was imperative that Sunset focus all his attention on smelling the new wonderful scents and exploring all the features of the magical land. Jilted Midas came up to Eve for attention. The large, dark brown dog rested his chin on her knee as he gazed into her eyes.

"I don't think I have ever been looked at with such absolute adoration," said Eve joyfully.

"You'll pay for it," Naiya said impishly.

"I'll pay for it?" Eve asked as she scratched Midas's ears. Sunset had finished his inspection of the area and came to retrieve his playmate. Midas jumped at the chance to chase Sunset around the yard. Eve realized that Midas had left her with a slobber-soaked pant leg to remember him by. She looked at Naiya with understanding. "Oh, is this my payment?"

"Yes. I call it the Midas touch."

"Wow. It really soaked through."

"Sorry!" Naiya laughed. "I should have warned you, but I needed you to experience it just once. People think I'm so mean because I won't let my sweet dog rest his head on my lap when I'm in the middle of workday. But they don't realize that I will have to spend the rest of my day with wet pants. I love him but it's gross. At home, in the evenings he gets plenty of time to snuggle with me, preferably with a towel on my lap."

"He's really adorable. And I'm so happy that Sunset enjoys playing with him. I've been feeling guilty that Sunset doesn't have another dog to play with at home. I considered the possibility of getting a second dog but I'm not sure I'm prepared to double down on the dog hair."

"Yes, living with a dog that sheds is like living in a completely different ecosystem. I don't think other people understand the exponential increase in vacuuming and laundry that we have to do."

Eve was beginning to feel like a parent who was so obsessed with her child's life, she forgot that she had one herself. *Okay, what do people talk about besides how cute their dog is?... Work!*

"Did you always know you wanted to be a veterinarian?" Eve asked.

"Not exactly. I was ten when my very strict parents informed me, yes — informed me, that I was going to be a doctor. I agreed on the condition that I could be a doctor for unicorns. But, unfortunately, I did not get accepted into the veterinary medicine program for mythical creatures, so this was the next best thing. Of course, I don't think this is what my parents had in mind when they put me on the doctor track. I think they expected me to tend to millionaires at un upscale hospital, not tending to horses in what they call 'the great unknown.' Of course, maybe if they bothered to visit, it wouldn't be so unknown."

"Where are you from originally?"

"Sonoma, California. You know, the known world."

"Wine country? Oh, please tell me that they taught you how to make wine in grammar school. I have a vineyard and no idea what to do with it!"

"I know you have a vineyard. I've had my eye on it the last couple of years. I mentioned it to Wes, but he said I shouldn't bring it up because it frustrates you."

Eve laughed. "It does frustrate me! I really want to take advantage of the fact that I inherited a vineyard. I want to make wine, but I need to get the hotel up and running before I try to add another gigantic project to my list. I'm looking forward to it, but right now it's infuriating to think of all those beautiful grapes falling to the ground. It's such a waste!"

"Well, I'm not an expert by any means, but I have spent plenty of time around vineyards. In Sonoma, a lot of my clients with horses also owned vineyards. And one thing I know is that if those vines are neglected, those grapes are not falling to the ground."

"They're not?"

"No. They're getting devoured by insects. So, they're not going to waste, if that makes you feel any better."

"Kind of… maybe… I don't know. So, in order to harvest the grapes next year, I'm going to have to figure out how to take care of the insects. That's a whole other thing to worry about!"

"Exactly."

"So, Naiya, do you want to go into the wine business with me? After all, you already have more knowledge than I do." Eve turned serious. "I know I just said that as a joke, but I think I'm serious."

"I would be interested. That sounds fun and challenging. But we would have to hire at least one person who actually knows what they're doing."

"Definitely."

On the drive home Eve was excited that she was cultivating a new friendship. The happiness it brought her almost masked the pain and guilt she felt leaving her dog behind.

Chapter Four

Gil Dancer was the first guest to arrive on early Wednesday afternoon. Ramon and Eve walked out to the parking lot to meet him.

"Nice to finally meet you, Gil," Eve said as she shook his hand. Eve's first impression was that Gil looked more like an old-fashioned adventurer rather than a modern-day restauranteur. "I've heard so many good things about you and your diner. Ramon told me that your wife wasn't coming out to stay with us."

"No, she has to work during the days and wants to stay home with the dogs at night. So, she sent me out here all by my lonesome."

"Well, I'm glad you could make it."

"I'm excited to see the old place again, and to stay here. As a young kitchen worker, I never thought I would actually get to stay at the hotel one day. I'm so happy that you've restored the place. For the last 25 years, I have driven by knowing it was abandoned, just sitting here, neglected. It broke my heart a little. I actually looked into the possibility of buying it, but I couldn't get anywhere with Mr. Thorton's people. I'm sure, even if I did, it would have been out of my price range."

Ramon and Gil started chatting as Eve caught sight of a blue crossover driving up the driveway. The car parked and three people exited.

"You must be Tom, Julie and Ben," Eve said before introducing herself and welcoming them. Tom and Julie were one of those couples that just looked like they went together. They both had the same color gray hair, were both fit and tanned and were both dressed in fashionably sporty clothes. Their son, Ben, on the other hand, looked like he could use a little more exercise and exposure to the sun. He wore a wrinkled T-shirt that read "An apple a day will keep anyone away if you throw it hard enough."

Eve asked Julie and Tom if they remembered Gil and Ramon. They admitted that they remembered Gil, but weren't sure about Ramon. Ramon explained that he had only briefly worked at the original hotel but now works at the current reincarnation.

Ben looked around at the wide-open spaces surrounding the hotel. Eve was expecting a comment on the serenity and beauty of the property, but instead Ben said, "Is there even Wi-Fi out here?"

"Yes," Eve assured him. "We have Wi-Fi. I also went to great lengths to ensure that the property has good cell phone reception. After all, I'm modern gal."

"I do not believe it is modern to use the term 'gal'," said Ramon teasingly.

Eve laughed. "Point, Ramon."

Ben finally noticed Eve. He gave her a once over with his eyes as he said, "So, if you have such good cell reception, maybe you should give me your number."

Eve had determined very quickly that, other than being of a similar age, she had nothing in common with Ben. She was not flattered by his sudden interest in her.

"Your mom has it," Eve said succinctly to end that line of inquiry. But she needed not worry about Ben's prolonged interest in her as he had already become distracted by something else. He walked around to the back of Gil's old pickup truck to admire a pair of guns in the back window gun rack.

"Bolt action rifle and a shot gun?" Ben asked.

"Yes. Nothing fancy, just my hunting guns," Gil answered.

"Cool. I like to go to this big indoor gun range in Vegas. They let you shoot machine guns."

"There used to be a shooting range here, back in the day," said Tom to his son.

"It's hot," Julie said irritably to her husband and son. "Can you two get your bags so we can go in?" She looked annoyed with her companions as she held what looked like two heavy suitcases.

Eve noticed Tom roll his eyes. To avoid the eruption of a marital dispute, Eve quickly said, "Yes, let's get you settled into your rooms. Let me help you with at least one of those." Eve gently pried one of Julie's suitcases from her hand before she could deny Eve's assistance. "Follow me."

She led the group into the hotel. She expertly hid the thrill she felt at checking in her very first hotel guests. Tom and Julie went into their room to unpack. Ramon took Gil on a tour of the hotel and property. Ben chose to stick with Eve. She used the opportunity to practice her hotel history spiel, explaining her personal connection to the property. Ben seemed uninterested in the history but perked up when she mentioned "personal connection." He took that as an opportunity to start asking her personal questions.

"I have to go out to the stables," Eve said as a means to extract herself from the conversation. It did not work.

"I'll go with you," Ben said quickly and once again followed her.

As they walked along the path to the stables, Eve continued to play gracious hostess and said, "So, Ben, what do you do?" Although secretly, she did not care for that question and would not use it if she was being truly tactful. She had always thought it was rude to ask someone's profession in that way, as if a person's work was the sum of their personality.

But Ben was happy to field the question. "I test video games before they launch to work out the bugs and glitches" he said a bit pompously. "I do it for all different studios. I really try to get the gigs where they're adding content to their existing map since I have the experience on that game, and I know how it should work already. When it's completely new material, it's harder to isolate the technical issues."

"Does that pay well?" Eve asked yet another question she would not normally ask in polite conversation.

"I do okay," Ben said proudly.

When they reached the stables, Eve felt a little guilty for taking pleasure in Ben's sudden discomfort. Ben's overbearing confidence vanished as she introduced him to Wes. Ben did not try to hide his instantaneous and severe dislike of Eve's strikingly handsome horse wrangler. As Eve talked to Wes about the plans for the group's horseback riding adventure the next morning, Ben walked off without a goodbye.

On Eve's way back to the hotel she spotted Julie walking around the pool and detoured to check in with her.

"Hello, Julie. What do you think of all the renovations?" Eve held her breath. She hoped that the employees of the old Arizona Sunset Ranch Hotel would like the changes she had made to the new Route 66 Ranch Hotel.

"I love them. I love them all. The pool looks amazing, and our suite is gorgeous. And I looked at Ben's room also, and wow. I must admit, it is so much fancier than when I worked here a million years ago."

"That makes me so happy, thank you. I had a lot of fun decorating all the rooms."

"Were you an interior decorator before you inherited the hotel?"

"Oh no. I can't even imagine the thought of having to please the different tastes of picky people. But being able to decorate every room in this hotel how I wanted was a dream come true. And I tried to make every guest room different."

"I would love to see the others if I could."

"Of course! Before anyone else arrives, I'll give you a tour. I love any opportunity to admire them myself."

As they walked to the hotel, Eve asked, "Were you born and raised in the Sandmat area?"

"No, my dad moved us here after my mom died. I was a teenager. I hated that he moved me out to the sticks. But looking back, I realize how tough it must have been for him, raising a teenage girl by himself. He needed help. We moved out here because my dad's best buddy from the war was a sheriff's deputy out here. He and his wife had a brood of kids so, it wasn't that much more work for them to throw me in the mix. My dad got a job working for the railroad and we lived in a little cabin on their property. It was a pretty good set up." Julie laughed as she reminisced, "And when I got the job here, I was so proud. I felt so grown up!"

During their tour of the rooms, Eve told Julie more about the changes she had made to the original hotel buildings. She told her about the places she had found some of the antiques and how she had a lot of the other furniture custom made for the hotel by a local artisan. She also made sure to give a lot of credit to her contractor. He deserved that.

Eve was happy to find someone that was keenly interested in all the work that had gone into restoring the buildings. She loved showing off her hotel. "And now there is central heat and air conditioning, and Wi-Fi," she added.

"I must admit, the Wi-Fi doesn't mean much to me,

but Ben would die without it."

"Well, I suppose he needs it for his job."

"His job?"

"His job testing video games."

"Did he really tell you that was his job?"

"Yes. Why? Does he not do that?"

"Oh, he does it, but it's not a job. He does it for free. Apparently, they don't have to pay when there are people like my son who get on waitlists to do it for fun. He does it just to have the chance to be the first to check out a new game. But as far as a job, no, he doesn't have one of those at the moment."

Eve regretted bringing it up. She didn't want Julie getting any more frustrated with her family. They had been having such a nice moment before that.

But before she could change the subject to something more pleasant, Julie said, "I'm sorry my son lied. I'm sure he was just trying to impress you. He doesn't often meet attractive single women his age."

"How did you know I was single?"

"No wedding ring," Julie said simply.

"But I could have a boyfriend." *I don't, but I could!* Eve exclaimed inside her head.

Julie laughed. "Oh, that wouldn't stop Ben." Julie then thanked Eve for the tour and excused herself to rest and freshen up.

Chapter Five

Loretta hurried across the lobby to Eve and gasped, "There's a weird man outside. I think he's coming in."

"Is he one of our guests? Is he carrying luggage?"

"He has a big ol' canvas duffel bag. Big enough to put a body in. That might be what's in there. He looks like a grave robber."

The front door opened, and a tall thin man walked in.

"Was you checking in here?" Loretta asked fiercely.

Eve thought how Loretta was more of the hotel's guard dog than Sunset would ever be. Eve quickly tried to rectify the suspicious nature in which the man had been greeted. "Hello, welcome," she said. "I'm Eve. Are you perhaps Sterling?"

"Yes," he said simply as he looked around the lobby.

Eve understood why Loretta was immediately wary of this man. Sterling had intense angular facial features highlighted by a significant scar on his right cheek and jaw. That, with the oversized stained duffel bag he was holding, gave him the look that Eve associated with news stories that mentioned "lone gunman." If he had been a random stranger who had wandered into the lobby of the hotel, Eve may have joined Loretta in her discomfort. But Eve had invited this man here and she was loathe to judge a book by its cover. Propelled by her natural desire to be a good hostess, she cheerily guided him to the reservation counter and checked him into his room.

As she rattled off the events of the next few days and the list of the other guests that had already arrived, Sterling remained quiet and continued to look around the hotel. Eve could not discern whether he was impressed or bothered by the changes she made to the building, as his expression did not change once. Perhaps he was completely uninterested. She walked him to his room and was happy to hear the front door open downstairs so she could excuse herself. Sterling stoically but politely thanked her before closing his door.

After Sterling's arrival, Loretta had stationed herself on the front porch, apparently keeping an eye out for any more weirdos. She must have decided that these two new arrivals did not fall into that category. Loretta was carrying armloads of their luggage and talking happily with the woman as they entered. Eve hurried down the stairs to meet them.

Eve quickly learned that her new guests were Annabelle Sheridan and her father, Walter Flint. Annabelle proved to be as amiable as she had been on the phone. She was also incredibly stylish and not shy about bringing a lot of luggage. Loretta had retrieved Roxie from the kitchen and the two went out to the car to bring in the rest of Annabelle's suitcases.

Roxie started carrying the luggage up to their rooms. Loretta asked Annabelle, "You want me to pull your car around and park it in the lot?"

"That would be fantastic," Annabelle replied. "Thank you," she said as she handed Loretta her car keys.

As Eve welcomed and chatted with Annabelle, she took turns looking at her and at her father to include him in the conversation. He was quiet and distant, avoiding eye contact with her and looking around at the room. At first, she self-consciously thought he didn't approve of her changes to the building that was his home for so many years, but she started to sense that wasn't the case. He seemed a little confused. She got the sense that Walter was struggling with some level of dementia. Annabelle had mentioned that her father was depressed, but not that he was suffering from memory issues. Eve wondered if Annabelle was unaware or possibly in denial.

Walter quietly walked off and sat on one of the leather couches in the middle of the lobby. Eve was so happy she had kept those beautiful old leather couches. Even if Walter did have problems remembering things, he probably felt at home sitting on the old couches that he must have sat on thousands of times over the years.

Annabelle joined her father and Eve brought them cucumber water. Eve sat and chatted with them. Eventually, they were joined by Ramon and Gil, and then Tom and Julie. Eve was delighted at the reunion thus far.

When Sterling walked down the stairs to join them, Eve thought it was bizarre that he brought his duffel bag, but no one else seemed to register it as strange. Ramon, Gil, and Tom all got up to shake Sterling's hand and welcomed him to the fold. Sterling walked over to Walter and also shook his hand.

"Nice to see you again, Mr. Flint," Sterling said before setting his duffel bag on the ground next to where he sat.

"Do you remember everyone, Dad?" Annabelle asked.

Walter nodded noncommittally. It was not apparent whether he remembered or whether he was going through the motions.

"Mr. Flint, do you remember how you were so strict on us but Annabelle could get away with anything?" Tom joked.

The group chuckled.

"I did get to run around like a wild child, didn't I?" Annabelle agreed. "Hey, those were the perks of being the boss's daughter," she said as she squeezed her father's hand.

"You were a good kid," said Walter. "The others needed to be kept in line. I remember. You think I don't remember, but I remember. The maids always trying to sneak over to the cowboy bunkhouse."

Everyone roared with laughter at that memory.

"That is so funny that you remember that, Mr. Flint!" exclaimed Julie. "Those other girls I worked with were troublemakers, it's true. But I was an angel."

Eve noticed that Tom slightly rolled his eyes as he opened his mouth to say something. Just in case it was a prelude to marital bickering, Eve decided to interject.

"So, I think we're just waiting for Millicent Buchanan," she said.

Her change of subject worked. Tom's countenance changed from one of disapproval to excitement. "Battleax Buchanan is coming?" he said happily.

"I forgot about that name! Old Battleax," said Julie.

"Hey, be respectful," said Gil. "I always was. I always called her Mrs. Battleax. Behind her back of course."

"She was a tough lady," said Sterling.

"Oh no, now I'm getting worried," said Eve.

"You shouldn't," said Annabelle. "The others may have been scared of her, but she was always 'Aunt Millie' to me."

"And she's probably softened up in her old age," suggested Julie.

"So, after Millie gets here, that's everyone?" asked Annabelle.

"Yes, that's it," said Eve. "Unfortunately, I couldn't locate everyone but I contacted a few other people. They were unable to come or never responded."

"So, no Hazy Daisy or Big Bob?" asked Gil.

"Did everyone have a nickname?" asked Eve.

"Of course. And mine was obviously Good Lookin' Gil."

As each person belted out a laugh in response, Gil looked around with a mock hurt expression and said, "It wasn't THAT funny."

"I don't know about a Big Bob, but I did contact a Daisy Malone, but she never got back to me. She worked with you in the kitchen, correct?" she asked Gil.

"Yes. Poor Daisy, she got all the grunt work. She was our resident potato peeler. She was an odd girl living in her own fantasy world. She fell in love with any boy that gave her the slightest attention, so I tried to keep my distance. She was painfully socially awkward."

"Oh, I remember Daisy," said Annabelle. "I liked her! She was my friend, the closest thing I had to a peer here. I remember thinking the fact that I had an adult friend must mean I was really mature, but, of course, I wasn't. Daisy must have been quite immature for her age. At ten or so years my senior, she was really on par with me emotionally."

"Daisy was a simple girl that was just too trusting. She believed everything anyone ever told her," said Sterling. "I think you were her only real friend here," he added to Annabelle.

"She stopped working here not too long after you left for boarding school," said Gil. "I wonder if she felt lonely after you left. But honestly, she wasn't the best worker in the world," Gil added. "I always wondered why Battleax kept her on, but I think the fact that she didn't fire Daisy was proof that she was a big softie under all her bluster. I think she didn't want Daisy to have to make it in the real world."

"This wasn't the real world?" asked Eve.

"We were definitely insulated here," said Tom.

"And what about Big Bob?"

The group started talking about the nice large cowboy that worked here for a few years in the mid-seventies. Eve explained that she had a hard time locating information on all the old ranch hands and the ones she did find were otherwise occupied. In the end, she had no old ranch employees showing up. She took this as an opportunity to let everyone know that Buck, Millicent's husband who had been the ranch foreman for over 30 years, had passed away. Therefore, Millicent was coming alone.

"Speak of the devil. I see a car coming up the driveway," announced Ramon who had stationed himself at the front window by the reception desk.

Ramon went outside and shortly thereafter was opening the door for a stout, strong woman with her gray hair pulled into a bun. She was tightly clutching her bags in her hands. Eve was quite certain that Ramon had offered to take her luggage, so she must have refused. She had the air of a woman who was used to doing things herself and would be offended if you offered her too much help.

Eve realized this new endeavor of hers was going to be an interesting experiment in learning how to deal with all sorts of different personalities. The navigation of properly treating people was a complex business. As a child, Eve thought being nice to people was simple, you just treated others as you wanted to be treated. As she got older, she realized it was far more problematic than that. Everyone was so very different and wanted to be treated differently. Today, for example, Annabelle gladly took the help of both bellhop and valet amenities whereas Millicent looked like she would be appalled to avail herself of those same services.

Once Millicent was in and had set down her bags, she-- as all the others had done-- looked around the familiar building. Eve welcomed her and reintroduced her to the group of people from her past. Millicent looked at everyone and with a frown said, "Y'all got old."

Perhaps she hadn't softened up, Eve thought.

Millicent turned back to Eve. "I want to see what you did to my kitchen."

Eve nervously chuckled as she guided Millicent to the

kitchen. She held her breath as she opened the door to let Millicent in. Would the property's long-time cook disapprove of the changes? Eve had found retro looking appliances to replace the old ones. She had been very proud of herself in keeping the old-fashioned look of the kitchen while modernizing it. Eve felt silly being so concerned, but this had been Millicent's kitchen for decades. Mr. Thorton had built and owned the property, but he was only here a fraction of that time. Millicent and Walter were two of the people that spent a significant portion of their lives here. She innately respected their opinions.

"Nice," Millicent said as she nodded seriously.

Eve had just met this woman, but she was quite certain that her one-word comment should be accepted as high praise. Eve was filled with satisfaction. The next few days were going to be perfect; she just knew it.

Chapter Six

"Welcome," Eve said to the group convened in the dining room. "There are just a few formalities I want to get out of the way before we start dinner. In front of each of you is a schedule of the events for the next couple of days. Underneath that is a contact sheet with all of your cell phone numbers. There is fairly good cell phone reception throughout the property. So, if you choose to explore, please make sure you have your phone on you and –"

"So, if there's a shooting range, can we shoot while were here?" Ben interrupted enthusiastically.

"No, I'm sorry. The old shooting range is just a wasteland of rusty cans. I have put cleaning that on the bottom of my to do list."

"Oh no," Gil cried melodramatically, "my past has come to haunt me!"

Eve looked at him questioningly.

"It was my job to clean up the cans when I went out to deliver the food to the ranch hands. But when the shooting range closed down, I figured I didn't have to do it anymore." Gil looked at Eve. "I'm so sorry. The laziness of my youth has caught up with me and I left a mess for you to deal with. That is unacceptable. I'll go out first thing tomorrow morning and clean them up."

Eve laughed. "You will do no such thing, Gil. I will not have my guests working while they're here."

"It doesn't matter anyway," said Ben. "I don't care about some rusty cans. That won't stop me from shooting."

"I'm afraid I will be the one stopping you from shooting," Eve said to Ben soberly. "I ask that no one does any shooting on my property, not even at the old range." Then she directed her attention to the group in general and returned to her speech. "As you will see on the schedule, I have history interviews scheduled with each of you throughout the next few days, as well as group activities, and of course, the most important part– meals."

"You may have to keep reminding me not to go make the meals," said Millicent. "It is quite strange being here and not being the one cooking. I keep thinking I need to get up and go to the kitchen."

"Well, I certainly won't feel compelled to clean the rooms!" said Julie.

Everyone laughed.

"When do you want our pictures?" Sterling asked Eve.

"Thank you for asking that. I would love it if you could all give me your photographs after dinner tonight," replied Eve. "I will be scanning them while you are here and I will return them to you before you leave. At least, I hope that I will be able to get it all done in the next few days. I'm not as young and fast as I used to be."

"Hey, we're all a lot older than you," barked Millicent.

"I'm not," muttered Ben.

Millicent rolled her eyes.

"Growing older has its challenges, but it also has its benefits," said Ramon to Ben.

"Like what?" asked Ben, apparently immune to Millicent's eyerolls, of which he received another.

"Wisdom, appreciation, understanding," said Ramon philosophically before adding, "and discounts, do not forget all the discounts!"

"And you need them too!" said Millicent. "Nowadays everything costs an arm and a leg."

"I know," agreed Ramon. "It is horrible. I remember when things only cost an arm."

Eve led the group's laughter after which she said, "He's here all week, folks!"

"Well, I used to hate getting old, but I decided to love it," said Julie. "Unlike most people, I embrace it. I truly feel blessed to be old and getting older. I used to hate every new spot, every new wrinkle. But then I remembered that my mom would always say that her few gray hairs were badges that she had earned. So, I started thinking that way. Now, I consider every new wrinkle as an accomplishment showing that I have lived. I learned to love getting older because that's the goal. After all, there's only one alternative. I feel sad that my mother died young and didn't get to see more gray hairs. So, I love all my gray hair on her behalf."

"That's beautiful, Julie," said Eve. "I will endeavor to think along those same lines."

"Yes, that is a lovely sentiment," agreed Annabelle. "But I personally will go to my grave as a blonde. If I have the ability to retain just one aspect of my youth, I'm going to take it!"

Chapter Seven

That night after dinner, while the others were relaxing and mingling in the lobby, Millicent helped Eve organize everyone's pictures using the tables in the dining room. Each picture was labeled with a sticky note on the back with the approximate date of the photograph and the name of the person the photograph belonged to so that Eve could return it to the appropriate person.

Millicent was amazing when it came to determining what year and season a picture was taken. Millicent's own photographs were already marked on the back with the names of people and the years, sometimes the specific dates. But the rest of the photographs, most of them being Sterling's, needed to be labeled. Eve was so thankful for Millicent's attention to this project. She could be a tough lady, as the others had warned her, but when she was looking at the pictures, she softened. She became particularly emotional when looking at pictures of her late husband. At one point, Millicent was so overcome with emotion, Eve heard her mutter, "I would do anything for that man."

While working on the picture project in the dining

room, Eve listened to the others talking in the lobby. Since she was so engrossed in the old photographs, she only registered snippets of conversation that wafted in from the large opening between the two rooms. Ben mentioned something about Bluetooth to which Ramon replied that he preferred Green Fingernail. Then she heard Gil say, "It's a joke." A little later she heard Annabelle laughing and saying, "I was so excited to actually go somewhere, I got a manicure before I came!"

"It'll be nice to be here and not have to be the cook for once," Millicent said, jarring Eve out of her daze. "The brats can all complain about someone else's cooking for once."

"They used to complain?" Eve asked.

"All the time. Just the employees, not the guests. The guests who were paying for their food liked it. But the little brats who were getting their room and board for free, they were the ones who always complained. When I first started working here, I tried to make them happy, but you know what they say: you can't please all the people all the time. So, I just stopped caring. I realized that they all wanted the same thing."

"If they all wanted the same thing, wouldn't it have been easy to appease them all with that same thing?" Eve asked.

"No, because what they all wanted was for me to make them food exactly like their mommy had made them."

Eve laughed.

"I'm not kidding. And it didn't even have to be good food. If their mommy used to make the most disgusting watery macaroni and cheese – that's what they wanted. So, little by little I got meaner and meaner and everyone finally shut up about it – to my face at least!"

Eve laughed again, happy that Millicent was opening up to her. She walked over to the table that had been reserved for the photos from the 1980s.

"Who is this little boy?"

"Our son Christopher."

"Oh, I didn't know you had any children."

"We tried to conceive for years, but it never happened. Then my sister in Iowa knew of a baby that needed a home, so we got baby Christopher, and he grew up here on the ranch."

"I am so sorry that I did not extend an invitation to him!"

"That's okay. He wouldn't have been able to make it anyway. He's a fire chief in New Mexico and this week is their fire school for the entire county. He teaches classes, so he can never get away this time of year."

"Well, please let him know that he is always welcome to come and see his childhood home."

Millicent pulled out a picture from her purse and showed Eve the photo of a handsome, smiling man in fire turnouts. "That's Christopher," she said proudly.

"Wow! The firefighters here don't look like that," Eve said. "Any chance he wants to move to Sandmat? He's like a calendar fireman. Do they have a calendar where he's from? If so, he must be on every month!" Eve knew she was laying it on a bit thick, but it was worth it to see the smile on Millicent's face. Plus, she wasn't lying, the man was incredibly good looking.

By the end of the project, Millicent had organized all the pictures in chronological order, so Eve could scan them in that sequence and see the changes in the hotel and property through the years. Millicent then joined the others in reminiscing. Ramon took the lead on taking care of the group as Eve went into her office to start scanning the pictures.

She started at the beginning, scanning the earliest photos. Unfortunately, there were no pictures from the 1950s in this compilation. Her only guest who had been here at that time was Walter, but it appeared that he had not been a shutterbug. The earliest pictures were the ones that Annabelle had brought beginning in 1962 when her mother, Constance, started working at the hotel. At year 1966, Millicent's collection increased the amount of photographs. Most of the current hotel guests had worked here in the 1970s, so the majority of pictures were from that decade, especially the mid to late 70s. The Constance and Millicent picture collections continued into the 80s and 90s when the building was no longer a hotel, only a vacation home for Mr. Thorton.

Eve was only up to scanning the pictures from the late 60s but her thoughts had turned to those years after the hotel had closed, when the ranch remained in operation and the vineyard was added to the property. The time that Walter, Constance, Buck, and Millicent were the only employees. *Other than the cowboys,* Eve thought. *And the… the… grapeboys? What do you call the people tending to the grape vines?* Eve realized she was getting deliriously tired. She forced herself to finish scanning the pictures from the 1960s before she couldn't keep her eyes open any longer.

Chapter Eight

After breakfast the next morning, the guests convened on the veranda for their scheduled outing to go horseback riding. Eve had been concerned since she only had six available horses but eight guests, nine if she counted Ramon, but in the end it had worked out perfectly. Annabelle suggested that her father stay behind, as long as someone stayed with him, to which Ramon gladly volunteered. Ben said that he "didn't do horses" and didn't want to spend his day "following around some pretty boy cowboy in the hot sun." Eve had been a little concerned that Ben chose to stay at the hotel because she was staying, but that left six riders for the six horses, so she was happy.

The six horseback day trippers followed Eve out to the stables. Halfway there, Annabelle announced that she had forgotten her hat and she headed back to the hotel. When the rest of the group arrived and congregated in the tack room, Eve explained to them that Wes would be their guide for the day.

"I'll be there in just a minute," Wes's voice called out from the opening on the other side of the building that led out to the horse pasture.

While waiting for Wes, Eve stood in front of her equestrians for the day: Sterling, Tom, Julie, Millicent, and Gil. She was about to fill the silence by thanking them again for coming when she heard Wes's footsteps behind her. Eve's words caught in her throat as she saw the facial expressions of her guests completely change on Wes's arrival. All of them looked like they had just seen a ghost, or a monster, or something else truly disturbing.

Eve quickly turned around to make sure it was indeed Wes that was behind her and not the big bad wolf. It was Wes, looking as handsome and affable as ever. She turned back to her guests who continued to exude an air of discomfort as they turned from one to the other exchanging peculiar expressions. Wes didn't seem to notice as he began his welcome speech and introduction to horseback riding. As he asked the group about their experience level and when the last time they were on a horse, the enigmatic tension dissipated.

Happily eager for her adventure, Annabelle arrived wearing a huge grin and a red cowboy hat that perfectly matched her pants. Eve stayed for a while and watched Wes at work, feeling very proud of herself for hiring him.

She then wished the group a good ride and headed back to the hotel. She entered the back door to the dining room. She noticed Ben had made himself at home in the lobby. He had headphones on, so he hadn't heard her come in. She ducked out of sight to the dining room table that Ramon and Walter were sitting at. Ramon had spread out some of the old photos on the table in front of Walter.

Eve sat at the table and said, "You worked here longer than anyone Walter. I bet you know everyone in those pictures."

Walter looked up at Ramon and Eve and then to the pictures a few times before saying, "That's Buck." He pointed to a man standing in front of a herd of cattle with a few ranch hands in the background.

"Did you know Buck?" Eve asked Ramon.

"He was Millicent's husband, so I knew of him, but he was the ranch foreman. I did not have any contact with him. I worked at the hotel and did not live out at the cabins, so I did not have occasion to run into him. I saw him once or twice, but I never spoke to him. I only remember that I regarded him as quite an intimidating man."

Walter continued to stare at that same photo and said, "You have to take out the trash. You can't feel bad about it. It's just trash. You have to get rid of trash. That's what you do with trash, you get rid of it."

Eve gave Ramon a concerned look, but Ramon looked unbothered. "Do you remember me, Mr. Flint? That was one of my jobs— taking out the trash. Do you remember that?"

Walter slowly nodded as he raised his head and stared out the back window towards the empty horse pasture.

"Where are the horses?" Walter asked.

"They're out on a trail ride right now. You'll see them out in the pasture later," replied Eve.

"Where's the killer?" asked Walter.

Eve again questioned Ramon with her eyes. Ramon shrugged his shoulders.

"Walter," Eve said attempting to get him out of his daze. "When you ran this hotel, did people call and make reservations, or did they just show up for the night?"

Walter stared at her with a glimmer of understanding in his eyes. This morning's current conversation was dispelling Eve's previous doubts about Walter's battle with dementia. He was noticeably struggling to remember simple things. Eve wondered if Annabelle realized the advanced stage of his condition.

"I believe it was your wife, Constance, that ran the hotel check-in?" Eve asked hoping the mention of his wife might get his memories jump started. It did.

"Constance checks in all the hotel guests," Walter said, suddenly alert. "She gets one of the boys to take their luggage up to their room. She is so good with people. Everyone loves her. After the guests meet Constance, they always choose to stay at our hotel when they come through this way. We have the best hotel. Constance makes it the best. I just pay the bills and keep everyone in line."

Eve was delighted to see that Walter's face of stone had cracked a slight smile. She wanted to keep him talking. She pointed to the closest photograph. It showed the old barn in the distance (in much better shape) and a few people engaged in some sort of activity.

"Do you know who these people are?" Eve asked, trying to keep the conversation flowing while Walter was talkative.

"Annabelle is a good shot," he said.

"That's right," said Ramon. "I remember now, when I worked here, Annabelle would practice target shooting all the time and enter competitions. One day, she brought back a trophy from a shooting competition in Prescott. She was so proud and so cute."

"Oh, is that the shooting range in that picture?" Eve took a closer look at the photograph. "Oh yeah, I see it now. Walter, did Annabelle win a lot of trophies?"

He nodded and repeated, "Annabelle is a good shot."

"And what about when Mr. Thorton and Genevieve, or Miss Cordova, came to the property?" Eve asked. She held her breath hoping Genevieve's name would shake loose some spectacular story about her great aunt that would help keep her memory alive.

"Mr. Thorton was a good man," Walter said as his face turned to stone once again. Eve had not failed to notice his tense had reverted to the past.

At that moment, Ben walked into the dining room and addressed Eve. "Oh, you're back."

Eve reminded herself that she needed to be kind to all

of her guests. Even though Ben was not her cup of tea, she needed to be hospitable. She decided to think of Ben's presence as a good thing. She could use it as an opportunity to practice being nice to people she didn't care for. After all, she owned a hotel now. She needed to learn how to successfully deal with all sorts of different personalities, pleasant and otherwise.

"Hello. Would you like something to drink? Cucumber water or iced tea?" She pointed out the dispensers on the bar.

"No."

Eve noticed that Walter was staring at Ben with a displeased look on his face.

"Let's go talk out on the veranda, Ben," she suggested. "It's such a beautiful day." Eve opened the back door and Ben was quick to follow her. They sat at one of the tables and faced the magnificent red rock cliff on the north side of the property. "Your parents both seem to like horseback riding. But you don't?"

"Not my thing. But my dad loves horses. He took care of the horses that some big magician in the 80s used for his crazy show. That's how he got into magic."

"Magic?"

"Oh yeah, my dad was a magician for a while. You know Vegas, it's crazy. Crazy people doing all sorts of crazy jobs."

"That is fascinating."

Ben beamed. Eve was sure that he had mistaken her interest in his father's past with an interest in Ben himself.

"Oh, yeah," he continued. "My mom was a showgirl for a while when she first moved to Las Vegas, from here I guess. You should see the pictures of the things she had to wear on her head. Crazy. But most of the time when I was growing up, my dad worked as dealer at different casinos and mom was a waitress and then she became a dealer like dad. But I remember going to one of my dad's magic shows when I was little. I thought it was so cool my dad was a magician."

"Do your parents ever talk about their time here?"

"Just that they met here. Then I guess my mom moved to Las Vegas and my dad followed her out there."

"Well, that's nice that they wanted to bring you here and show you where they lived and met."

"I think they mostly brought me 'cause they just didn't trust leaving me at the house by myself. So stupid."

"Oh. You live with them?"

"Yeah, it's just temporary. My roommates… It's a long story." Ben closed his eyes and shook his head as if to erase his currents thoughts. When he opened his eyes, he looked at Eve and said, "So, what about you? What's your deal?"

Eve had always loathed when a man tried to hit on her by saying "what's your deal." It infuriated her that, instead of thinking of something charming to say or something interesting to ask, he thought he could engage in conversation by putting all the pressure on her. Not only was she supposed to do all the talking and divulge all sorts of personal information about herself for the benefit of this lout, but she was also supposed to pick the topic, having to determine what 'deal' meant. Hearing those words always and immediately raised her ire.

What's my deal?! Eve screamed inside her head. But practicing her forced friendliness, out loud she said, "At the moment, I'm working on opening a hotel and learning as much about the history of the property as I can. That's why I invited all the old hotel employees here, so I can learn more about the workings of the original hotel. Speaking of which, I should get back in to speak with Walter some more."

She got up and walked into the dining room. She was annoyed that Ben was following her but when she sat down with Ramon and Walter, Ben continued to the lobby where he started playing video games again. She was happy to be rid of Ben's company but was disappointed in Walter's. He continued to look at the old pictures but didn't have anything more to say. It was frustrating to have Walter here in front of her, the man who had worked here longer than anyone else, and yet not be able to access all the information and memories in his head.

When Walter got antsy, stood up, and started walking, Ramon announced, "I guess we are going for a walk," as he followed Walter outside.

"Thanks, Ramon," Eve called out.

She decided to take the available time to go scan more photos, but when she walked into her office she remembered her query from the night before. She got on her computer to search for wine making terminology.

She had laughed at her tired self the night before when she suggested that the people who tend to grape vines at a vineyard might be called "grapeboys", but she didn't feel so stupid when she found out that they are actually called vinedressers. It conjured up a ridiculous image of someone arranging scarves and hats along the vines. She did a little more research and found that the vinedresser is the person who oversees the propagation, planting, pruning, and tending of grape vines whereas a viticulturalist is the agricultural professional who specializes in the science of grape cultivation and management. Then she came upon the term vigneron, a person who cultivates grapes for winemaking and works out in the vineyard. *Wait, isn't that the same as the vinedresser?* Then she found the term vineyardist as a person who owns or cultivates a vineyard. Then a vintner is a person who grows grapes and makes wine. *Okay, I knew that one.* AND... a vigneron is a person that is closely linked to the vine. *Linked to the vine? What does that mean? Wait, I already found vigneron... Maybe I'll just stick with grapeboys and grapegirls.*

Frustrated that her future wine making endeavor was confusing her simply with its terminology, she was happy to return to the thoughtless task of scanning pictures. But as she scanned, she couldn't help but remember the uncomfortable energy with the group in the stables earlier. The more Eve thought about the strange moment, a nagging uneasiness came over her.

Chapter Nine

At half past noon, Wes called Eve and told her that the ride was over and her guests were walking back to the hotel. She hurried to meet them at the back door and told them to get water or iced tea from the large receptacles on the bar in the dining room.

"Lunch will be served soon if you would like to stay here in the dining room," Eve said to the group.

"I'd like to check on my father. Where is he?" Annabelle asked.

"He's in his room taking a nap. Ramon and he went on a pretty lengthy walk earlier. Your dad is in good shape."

"I know," Annabelle laughed. "I always tell people that I have a hard time keeping up with him and they always think I'm being kind, but I'm dead serious. He is faster and more agile than me. And it's probably going to be worse after that horse ride." Annabelle comically walked out of the room exaggerating her sore muscles.

"I'm going to get cleaned up before lunch," said Julie. "I can't eat while wearing this much horsehair." She jauntily followed Annabelle out of the room. Eve noticed that the hours-long horse ride did not seem to physically faze Julie. As Julie walked by her son, who was still in his video gaming position on the couch in the lobby, she tussled his hair.

The rest of the group helped themselves to the offer of hydration and sat at tables in the dining room. Moments later, Ben walked in, told the group how "rough" they looked and started looking at the large pictures of the property that Eve had used to decorate the dining room walls. When she first moved into the old hotel and found a box with some old pictures of the property from its heyday, she was overjoyed. Of course, now that she had access to so many more photographs, she was going to need to buy more picture frames.

"Hey, this guy looks just like your cowboy," said Ben.

"Oh yeah, I know," Eve said. "It is quite the resemblance. I keep meaning to show Wes that picture. I asked Ramon if he knew him, but he said he didn't recognize him." Eve took the picture frame off the wall and turned to the others. "That was one of the many questions on my list of things to ask you all. So, do any of you remember this man?" She held up the photo close to them so they could see.

Instead of a simple yes or no answer, Eve was given a show of turning heads. Millicent, Sterling, Tom, and Gil took turns looking at each other. Eve was reminded of the strangeness she had sensed in the stables earlier. They must have noticed Wes's striking resemblance to this man. There was obviously a story connected to this ranch hand. She decided to wait out the awkwardness until someone answered her.

"That worm's name was Dirk Slagter," said Tom.

"Nobody liked him," said Sterling.

"Julie liked him," Tom said with a hint of jealous anger.

"He was a thief," said Millicent. "He was always stealing food, and I'm sure he was the scoundrel who took those cattle."

"A cattle rustler?" Ben asked, suddenly interested.

"Yes, I'm sure it was him and more importantly, Buck was sure it was him," Millicent said. "That boy was a vile, disrespectful, waste of a human being."

No wonder seeing Wes was a shock this morning, Eve thought.

"And Buck was the ranch foreman, correct?" Eve asked to encourage the flow of information.

"Yes," said Millicent. "After those cattle went missing, Buck felt responsible, so he insisted on paying for them. In the end, that scoundrel, Dirk, stole from me. Me! He took thousands of dollars from me and my husband."

"How long did he work here?"

"Not long at all. It didn't take long for everyone to figure out he was bad news," said Sterling.

"Did he get fired for the cattle rustling?" Ben asked. "Did he get arrested?"

"We could never prove he did it, but it ended up not mattering," said Millicent guardedly.

"Why?" asked Eve.

A suspiciously long moment passed before Tom said, "Because he didn't work here anymore."

"So, he did get fired," suggested Ben.

Another pause. "Not exactly," said Gil finally.

"He quit?" asked Eve.

"No," Millicent huffed.

"Then what?" Eve asked.

More strained silence. Gil was again the one to succumb to the task of filling the awkward quietness. "He died."

"Oh!" exclaimed Eve. "How old was he?"

"About twenty-five," said Sterling.

"How did he die? An accident?"

"He had a bad heart," Tom said nastily.

"Tom!" Millicent reprimanded him.

"Well, he didn't have a good heart," Sterling said,

coming to Tom's defense.

"He didn't have a bad heart," Millicent corrected. "Not physically anyway."

"I'd say it was in pretty bad shape after the bullet put a hole in it," Tom said wryly. The others looked at him with concern.

"Oh! Someone shot him?" asked Eve as she clutched her chest.

The four employees of long ago looked at each other for a few moments before Sterling broke the silence. "He was accidentally shot at the shooting range by a hotel guest."

"How horrible," Eve gasped. She waited for more information.

"No one knew who exactly, but the guests were long gone by the time the body was found," said Gil.

"Old Sheriff Weed was about to retire and had no interest trying to locate all the guests. He told us to close down the shooting range, so we did. And that was the end of it," said Millicent.

"Sheriff Weed?" Ben interjected. "No way, dude! Weed? Sheriff Weed? That's awesome."

Everyone ignored Ben's inappropriately jubilant outburst.

"Wow," Eve said somberly, "I had no idea. I was hoping to learn some interesting stories about the property, but I wasn't expecting that," she said as she hung the picture back on the wall.

Chapter Ten

After lunch, Eve went to her office and turned on her computer to scan photos, but she couldn't stop thinking about Dirk, the cowboy who looked so similar to Wes. They even wore similar cowboy hats. She reflected on Dirk's unfortunate end and shivered at the thought of Wes being shot by accident. She felt vindicated in her refusal to allow shooting on the property.

She kept thinking of how easily an accident like that could happen. But the more she thought about it, the less she believed herself. *How could that happen?* she wondered. Would Dirk have been standing near the targets while guests were shooting? A lone guest was left unattended at the shooting range? Wasn't it Sterling's job to monitor them? The scenario started to make less and less sense.

She abandoned her scanning project and pulled up the Sandmat Sentinel website. She had a subscription to the online newspaper that allowed her access to the archive of Sentinel editions going back to 1952. Thanks to the tech-savvy whiz kid who bought the Sentinel a few years back, the archive had been digitized and catalogued so that it was easy to search for anything. It was an amazing resource for Eve while researching the history of the area. She searched for Dirk Slagter. The fast, user-friendly website did not disappoint. It quickly pulled up an article, but the article itself was a disappointment. If you could even call two sentences an article.

The newspaper from 1977 read:

Accidental Death West of Sandmat
Juniper County Sheriff Weed has determined the death of ranch hand, Dirk Slagter, to be accidental. Slagter was found deceased on a ranch west of Sandmat on the 18th of August.

Eve shivered. Today was the 18th of August. The coincidence somehow made the 46-year time difference seem suddenly irrelevant. Something else about the date was familiar also… She walked across the lobby to her suite and found Genevieve's diary from 1977. She skimmed through it. *No, not this…* yes, she remembered now. It was a letter from Aunt Genevieve to Eve's mother, Minna, that Eve had read before. She opened the shoe box in which she kept the letters and found the one she was looking for. It was not dated August 18th, 1977, but just a few days later.

August 21st, 1977

Dearest Minna,

We are back in Arizona at last! It is a bit warm this time of the year therefore I am spending the lion's share of my time at the pool rather than horseback riding. It is so serene here. I wish you could visit. But you are a young adventurous lady and might find the peacefulness tiresome. Perhaps one day when you are older you will delight in the art of idleness as I do now. We have been here only one day, and I already feel far more relaxed. When Fergus and Leslie met us at the plane yesterday, at the property's air strip in the wide open spaces of the Arizona countryside, it felt like coming home. I believe this is the place that restores my sanity.

But it is not all fun and relaxation here at the moment. I have been busy —

There was more to the letter, but Eve got the information she was looking for: August 21st. Mr. Thorton and Genevieve had been here one day. They arrived on the 20th, only two days after Dirk was killed. Eve again briefly looked at Genevieve's diary from 1977. No mention of a death on the property. Eve assumed that Dirk's death was something the staff had kept from Mr. Thorton and Genevieve.

But the most important information was that — if the hotel staff cleared out the hotel a full week before Mr. Thorton's arrival, as she had read in a diary entry, then there were no guests at the hotel when Dirk was killed. A guest did not accidentally shoot Dirk, and the entire staff would have known that. As she had starting suspecting, she had been lied to.

As she distractedly looked at the clock on the wall, she realized that it was time for her first history interview. Annabelle had suggested that she and her father do their interview together so she could help jog her Dad's memory with her stories of growing up at the hotel and ranch.

After finding her interviewees and leading them back to the office, Annabelle and Walter got comfortable in the office chairs opposite Eve.

"Thanks for doing all this, Eve," Annabelle said. "It's really great to be back here and see the old place back in action. My mom would be thrilled. I have so many wonderful memories here, and I'm just having the nicest time."

"You are too kind! I feel bad that my main motivation was to use you all to get more information on the hotel."

"You shouldn't feel bad about that! That's a noble endeavor. A lot of people wouldn't bother to find out the history of the property they are renovating. I think what you're doing is wonderful, and I'm happy to be part of it. And Dad is too, right, Dad?"

Walter smiled kindly at his daughter but said nothing.

Eve turned on the recording app on her computer and begun the interview with the questions she had prepared last week. Annabelle happily talked about her childhood on the property. She was a great resource to tell Eve about the changes to the property over the years since her parents had lived there until 1998 and she had visited often.

After Eve exhausted her prepared questions and a few others she thought of as Annabelle spoke, she decided to ask about Dirk's death.

"Who?" was Annabelle's response.

"His name was Dirk Slagter. He was a cowboy here for just a short time in 1977. He was found shot to death out at the shooting range."

"How tragic! I didn't know that," said Annabelle. "Let's see, 1977… I would have been 13. I guess that it must have happened after I went off to boarding school."

Walter had been quiet during the interview thus far, but Eve had noticed that his eyes narrowed when she brought up Dirk.

"Do you remember Dirk, Walter?" Eve asked him.

"I… no," he said.

Or was it "I know," wondered Eve.

"Sorry, I don't know anything about it," repeated Annabelle. "And like I said I was probably off at school already, and my parents wouldn't have told me about something like that anyway. Right, Dad? You were always protecting me, weren't you?"

Walter lovingly smiled at her and said, "Yes."

"But you don't have to protect me anymore. Now, I protect you," Annabelle laughed. "Oh, that reminds me of another story! My dad protecting me… I was probably around 6 or 7 and I had just learned about the dangers of rattlesnakes. I was sure that I saw one in front of our cabin, and I ran inside and stayed there all day, I was too scared to go back outside. When my mom explained this to my dad when he came home from work, he went out and searched. He came back in and assured me that there was no rattlesnake out there, but I was still scared, too scared to sleep. So, Dad went out and searched again. He was gone for an hour or two. When he came back, he had a dead rattlesnake in his hand.

"I have often thought about that," Annabelle continued wistfully. "Looking back, I'm not even sure I really saw a rattlesnake, or any snake for that matter. I think it was probably just my childish fears playing tricks on me. But to set my mind at ease, my father scoured the land to find a rattlesnake to kill so that I would feel at peace that night. How sweet is that?" Annabelle looked to her father for any signs of remembrance, but Walter seemed engrossed in the bookshelves behind Eve.

Eve and Annabelle continued to pleasantly chat about all sorts of things. Eve had such a wonderful time talking with Annabelle, it made up for the fact that Walter didn't have anything to add at the moment. She was such a joy to be around and really added a gaiety to the events that would be lacking without her charms. Perhaps it was just because she had been the baby of the group, but everyone loved Annabelle.

Chapter Eleven

Although it was too early to be doing so, Eve was setting the tables in the dining room in preparation for dinner. She was feeling a bit overwhelmed at the hundreds of little things that needed to be done and was trying to keep up on things while she thought of them and had a free moment.

She heard the sound of footsteps approaching and looked up with her happy-hospitable-hostess-face. She was immediately disappointed in her inability to maintain her smile when she realized that it was Ben. Luckily, he did not notice since he was busy surveying the contents of the room.

"Have you seen my dad?" Ben asked hurriedly. "My mom is looking for him and I want to find him before she goes ballistic."

"He's at the horse pasture fence petting Tempest." She accompanied her answer by carelessly pointing out the window to a figure in the distance as she returned her attention to the place settings.

"Ugh. He left his phone in the room," Ben said as he made his way to the back door.

Eve thought it was good that Ben would be forced to take a short walk to retrieve his father, but she soon realized he had no intention of doing such a laborious task.

"DAD!" he bellowed from the open doorway.

How lazy are you? thought Eve as a voice from the entrance to the lobby startled her.

"And all this time, I thought I was your dad."

Eve and Ben both whipped their heads in the direction of the voice to find Tom standing there with an amused look on his face. They then both looked back to the now mysterious figure by the fence before once again resting their gazes on Tom.

As Eve's initial shock turned into understanding, she asked, "Then who's that?"

"Looks like Gil to me," Tom replied.

Tom was immediately proven correct as Gil turned towards them and started walking towards the swimming pool.

"Ben," Tom started in an admonishing fatherly tone. "I understand Eve confusing the two of us. After all, she just met us. But you? My very own son can't tell us apart?"

Eve was embarrassed that she recognized her new horse but was unable to recognize her new guests. Ben showed no signs of embarrassment.

"I guess all you old guys look alike," he said with waggish smile before remembering his task at hand. His smile vanished as he said, "Mom wants you, like ten minutes ago."

Tom's smile also faded as he sighed and said, "Okay."

As Tom and Ben walked out of the room, Eve thought about how much she liked both Tom and Julie and wondered why they didn't seem to like each other. But, having been raised by a single mother and having never been married herself, Eve fully admitted her ignorance to marriage's varied complications.

After finishing the table settings and refilling the water dispenser, Eve decided to sneak off to her suite for a moment to see if she looked as disheveled as she felt. When she entered the lobby, she came upon a woman standing in the middle of the room with her arms outstretched. The woman had her back to Eve, so she couldn't tell who it was. The longer she looked, the more certain she became that it was not one of her current guests. The woman seemed to be in the appropriate age range, but this woman was too thin to be any of her female guests and she was draped in a rainbow of gauzy materials.

"Hello? Can I help you?" Eve asked.

The woman turned around. "Oh, my apologies. I was just overwhelmed with the energy of being back here. I was filled with a restoration of youth."

Eve couldn't begin to think of what to say.

"You must be Eve. My apologies for my tardiness. Sometimes my traveling home takes me on alternative journeys."

What is happening right now? Eve thought. Aloud she said, "I suppose I must apologize to you because I am not sure who you are."

"I'm Daisy, of course. Daisy Malone."

"Oh yes, I do remember I left you a voicemail, but you never got back to me. I'm so sorry, I was not expecting you for this event."

"Expectations can change. It is the ebb and flow of life."

Eve again failed to find a response.

"I took a detour to Sedona," Daisy continued. "The vortexes overwhelmed us."

"Us?"

"Yes. I needed a spiritual overhaul and my home needed a new fuel pump."

"Oh, yes, those vortexes will do that," said Eve. At least she thought of a response this time. "Well, I do have rooms available it you would like to join the events for the next few days."

"It is not necessary. I can stay in my home. It is in the parking lot."

"I'm sure your home is lovely, but I insist on giving you a room while you stay here."

"Then, I am forever grateful," Daisy said with a bow.

Millicent walked into the room. "Daisy!" she exclaimed. "What are you doing here?"

Eve was impressed with Millicent's ability to recognize Daisy after 45 years, but she was unimpressed with her reaction. It was not at all welcoming.

"I decided to come to the reunion," Daisy replied simply.

"We weren't expecting you— Eve wasn't expecting you," Millicent said in a more subdued tone.

"It's fine," said Eve. "The more the merrier. There is plenty of room and plenty of food."

Millicent must have felt guilty for barking at Daisy, because after Eve checked Daisy into Room 1, Millicent offered to help get her settled in.

Chapter Twelve

It was an afternoon of relaxation and socialization. Eve scheduled it that way, or rather, not scheduled it that way. She also wanted to make sure her employees, especially Ramon enjoyed spending time with the old hotel staff. But her employees were such dedicated workers that Wes and Loretta insisted they had too many things to do to relax with the others.

Eve found it funny that the men and women had naturally separated. The ladies had convened in the lobby and the men were out on the veranda. All the men except for Ben. He had been stationed in one of the large leather lobby chairs engrossed in an online game with his headphones on. He seemed completely unaware of the presence of the women pleasantly chatting around him.

Julie was taking advantage of the all-female audience to vent her frustrations with the opposite sex. She had just inquired into Annabelle's relationship status. When Annabelle mentioned she had been divorced and single for the last eight years, Julie responded by saying, "Lucky you!" a little too enthusiastically.

Julie obviously sensed everyone's discomfort and a

slight blush showed on her cheeks. She checked to make sure her son wasn't listening, and she tried to explain her comment. "I just mean… it might be nice. I must admit, it would be nice to experience being single as an adult. I was so young when I got married."

She was met with silence, so she continued to explain herself. "Honestly, being tied to a man can be oppressive at times. They act like they are so much tougher physically than us but we're the ones having the babies. And they like to pretend that we are the emotionally sensitive ones when secretly we're constantly having to coddle their oversensitive egos. And because of those fragile egos they have to constantly prove they are tough, so they go and do stupid, stupid things even though we are perfectly capable of taking care of ourselves."

Julie's face had darkened but suddenly she smiled and forced a laugh as she said, "My theory is that all men's personalities are just a combination of part little boy and part old grump. For example, my son over there is 90% little boy and 10% old grump. Tom is about 75% old grump and 25% little boy. Mr. Flint is and always has been 100% old grump."

"That's not fair," said Millicent sternly. "Yes, he was very serious, but he had his moments. I would say he was only 97% old grump," she said with a twinkle in her eye.

When the group realized that the rigid Millicent had actually made a joke, they all started laughing in unison. Still chuckling at her father's expense, Annabelle looked out towards the veranda to check on him.

Ramon walked in from the kitchen. "I am so sorry to interrupt ladies, but I could not help but overhear your conversation. Pray tell, what is my ratio?"

Julie cocked her head to the side as she considered the question. "As far as I can tell, you're not normal. You're 50/50."

"Is that good?"

"I must admit, that's as good as it gets," Julie replied.

"You got one of the rare ones, Esperanza."

Esperanza beamed with pride as she lovingly admired her husband.

"Ramon, you are the perfect anomaly," said Eve.

"The Perfect Anomaly, that would be a good name for a band," said Roxie.

"Well, you ladies have fun, I believe I need to go start a band," said Ramon before he walked away to rejoin the men on the veranda.

Daisy was giggling at Ramon's comment until she saw Millicent glaring at her. She immediately stopped.

"What about you, Daisy? Are you married?" asked Julie.

"Widowed," Daisy replied simply and then added, "twice."

Eve felt so bad, but she wanted to keep things light, so she blatantly changed the subject. "Roxie, when Julie worked here, she had the same job you do," she said.

"You were a housekeeper?" Roxie asked Julie.

"Oh, we were called maids back then," said Julie. "The housekeeper was Mrs. Flint. She kept the house in order. She was our boss. She made sure that everything ran smoothly at the hotel. I thought about that years later, the fact that she was called the housekeeper and that was a very prestigious title."

"I know," said Annabelle. "One day I was watching a television show about some English manor house full of servants and I thought about the hotel here when I was little and how it was kind of similar. There was Millie, the cook; the team of maids; my mother, the housekeeper; and my father was kind of like Mr. Thorton's valet or butler."

"That's an interesting way to look at that," said Eve.

"But it really wasn't like that," said Millicent. "Maybe a little when Mr. Thorton was in residence. But he wasn't here all that often. It wasn't like we were anyone's servants; it was usually like it was our hotel and ranch.

Walter, Constance, Buck and I ran this place for years like it was ours. Especially Walter, he ran everything and knew everything." She looked at Annabelle. "He was a sharp man."

Annabelle smiled at Millicent and muttered, "Thanks."

"Well, it's pretty easy so far," Roxie said self-assuredly as she stood up. "I'm going to go help Mom," she said to Eve before opening the door that led to the basement.

After Roxie left, a scowling Millicent said, "I don't like confidence in children. They have no right to it. They do not have the experience or wisdom to own such confidence. They should at the very least have the self-awareness to know that they know nothing."

"Well, Roxie isn't a child. She's nineteen," said Eve coming to Roxie's defense.

"She's certainly not an adult," replied Millicent. "Nineteen is not an adult. Thirty-five is an adult." Millicent made a show of turning her head towards Ben. She stared at him as she said, "Most of the time."

Since Ben was playing video games with his headphones on, he was unaware that he had just been insulted. And since Ben was playing video games with his headphones on and wearing a T-shirt that read "Can't adult right now", no one bothered to disagree with Millicent's insinuation.

Millicent was not finished with her tirade of youth. "I know what young people think because I used to be young. But they don't understand the condition of being old. At that age, they think of themselves as adults but to us, they are like children— babies really. They think they have all the answers, but they are just starting to figure things out. They don't realize that the same way they look at a toddler is the same way we look at them."

Time to steer the conversation back to hotel history, thought Eve. She didn't even care if it was obvious and abrupt.

"Oh, I wanted to ask you all a question about this picture." Eve pulled a picture from the top of a box she had sitting on one of the end tables. "What is going on here?" She handed the photograph to Julie.

"Oh!" Julie started laughing and handed the picture to Annabelle. "That's the cow plop at our company picnic!"

"A blast from the past!" exclaimed Daisy.

"I completely forgot about that!" said Annabelle with delight as she handed the picture to Millicent.

"I didn't," said Millicent, "because this is one of my pictures and I look through them regularly. I like remembering the old days."

"Okay, ladies," said Eve. "I'm going to need an explanation. What is a cow plop?"

"Oh, it's fancy," Julie said jokingly. "It's like the roulette table of the ranch world. You paint a grid of numbers on the ground in a cow pen and put the cow in there. Everyone bets on the location of where the cow is going to…"

"To what?" asked Eve. "Plop?"

"Exactly."

"And plop is…?"

"Poop."

"Oh, that is fancy!" exclaimed Eve as the women all started laughing so loud that Ben finally looked up at them in consternation and removed himself. As he walked up the stairs to his room, the ladies laughed even louder.

Esperanza excused herself to start preparations for dinner. Now that Eve was alone with only old hotel employees, she thought she would bring up Dirk.

"So, Millicent and the others were telling me earlier about Dirk, the ranch hand that got shot in 1977," Eve mentioned as casually as possible. She watched Daisy and Julie for signs of discomfort.

"What exactly happened?" Annabelle asked the others. "As I told Eve earlier, I don't know anything about it."

Millicent succinctly repeated the story that she and the others had told Eve earlier.

Eve turned to Julie. "What about you, Julie?" she asked. "Did you know Dirk?"

"No, I didn't know him. I remember that there was some accident, but I didn't know him. I think that the accident was why the shooting range closed down."

"I read in one of my Great Aunt Genevieve's diaries --" Eve began.

"She was such a nice lady, by the way," said Annabelle. "Sorry to interrupt. I just keep forgetting to tell you that."

"Yes, everybody liked Miss Cordova," said Julie.

"Even me," Millicent joked.

"Thank you, all. That is very nice to hear. She was very special to me which is why this place is so special to me," said Eve. She felt a tear forming and tried to fight it from falling. She regained her composure before continuing. "So, I've been reading Aunt Genevieve's diaries and... well, actually, before I get into that, I'd like to ask you something else. Do any of you know if Genevieve was in a relationship with Mr. Thorton? In her diaries, she doesn't mention him which is strange since her whole life revolved around him. He is noticeably absent from her stories."

"They were nothing but professional when I saw them together," said Millicent.

Julie, Annabelle, and Daisy agreed.

"Perhaps she felt it her duty to not disclose any personal facts about Mr. Thorton since he was her boss," suggested Julie.

"She may have even signed a nondisclosure agreement that included diary entries, who knows," said Annabelle.

"Unfortunately, the person that spent the most time with your great aunt, who knew her the best, was

Walter's wife, Constance," said Millicent. "I'm sure she could have told you a great deal about Miss Cordova."

Eve was suddenly crestfallen. She had been hoping the ladies had some juicy stories to tell about her great aunt and her boss, but no such luck. Back to the matter at hand. "Okay, so, in one of Genevieve's diaries she mentioned that the staff always cleared out the hotel guests one full week before Mr. Thorton's arrival."

"Oh yes, I remember that. Everybody loved those weeks. It was like a holiday," said Annabelle.

"It wasn't exactly like a holiday. It was a lot of work," corrected Millicent. "Extra cleaning, preparing for special guests, shopping for special food, but without the hotel in operation, we did have some extra time to do personal things."

"We always got an extra day off that week," said Julie. "I loved it."

"Yes, Constance was good about that," said Millicent. "She wanted the staff to be in good spirits when Mr. Thorton arrived so she arranged for them to have extra time off prior to his arrival. It worked like a charm."

"Oh, I remember," said Daisy. "Annabelle is right. When I heard Mr. Thorton was coming, I was so happy. The week between the hotel guests leaving and Mr. Thorton arriving was kind of like a holiday."

"The reason I asked," said Eve, "is because I was told that Dirk was accidentally shot by an unknown guest. But only two days after he was killed, my great aunt was here at the hotel with Mr. Thorton. So, there wouldn't have been any hotel guests here at the time Dirk was shot and killed."

As the four ladies took turns looking at each other, Eve was struck by how each of them had a completely different look on her face. Annabelle looked puzzled; Julie, anxious; Daisy, terrified; and Millicent, irritated.

"Fine," Millicent grumbled. "Everything we told you earlier was the truth, except for the guest part. But that is what was told to the sheriff at the time, so I thought we should stick with that version of events."

"But that means that if it wasn't a guest that killed him, it was someone here at the ranch. Didn't that concern you all?"

"No one knew what really happened," said Julie. "It could have been an accident. It probably was, so what would have been the point?"

The raucous sound of men enjoying themselves filled the hotel as the group from the veranda came in the back door and joined the ladies in the lobby. Eve's companions seemed eager to abandon the current topic of conversation and quickly welcomed the men. Julie even got up and greeted her husband with a kiss on the cheek before she slipped her arm into his. And Eve was amused to see Daisy fixing her hair and adjusting her skirt while trying to pretend that she was not staring at Sterling out of the corner of her eye.

Chapter Thirteen

All the other meals for the long weekend were buffets, but Eve wanted to have one served dinner, and tonight had been the night. All in all, Eve was happy with the turnout. Esperanza had created a limited menu and Eve had printed out the options so that her guests could review them and order from the table just like a real restaurant. It was an experiment for the future. Tonight, Loretta and Roxie acted as the wait staff, Wes played the part of Esperanza's assistant cook, and Eve ran back and forth between the kitchen and the dining room attending to odds and ends. She had forced Ramon to act as a guest and spend time with the other previous hotel employees.

After dessert, all the guests once again made themselves comfortable on the couches and chairs in the lobby. Ramon and Eve joined them after having been kicked out of the kitchen by Esperanza. She assured them it did not take six people to load a dishwasher. She told them to enjoy the reunion. Loretta, Roxie, and Wes agreed that they were more than capable to help clean up.

Ramon was his usual charming self and told the group an amusing anecdote about the trials and tribulations of being a young bus boy. Eve refilled after-dinner drinks for everyone.

A few others told some funny stories about working and living on the property. Eve finally sat down and was trying to remember all the details to each story, until she realized she would be recording the history interviews during the next few days and she would just need to remember to ask each of them to repeat their particular story.

A thud from the kitchen made everyone look around.

"Oh, it's just Ernest," Julie laughed.

"Ernest?" Eve asked.

"Do you not know about Ernest?" Tom asked with a smile.

"No," Eve said slowly.

"Then, I suppose it is our duty to introduce you to your resident ghost," Tom laughed.

"Oh no," said Ramon. "I am glad Esperanza is not here to hear this."

"Of course she isn't here," said Eve. "She's the one in the other room making the noises that people are mistakenly attributing to supernatural forces."

"It looks like we have ourselves a non-believer," Millicent said.

Eve couldn't tell if Millicent was joking or serious.

"Don't worry, Eve," Daisy said. "Ernest is a nice ghost. He only punishes the wicked. And the more wicked, the more he punishes."

Eve was pretty sure that Daisy was dead serious.

"Okay, okay," Eve relented. She could join in the fun. Plus, if the story of Ernest was part of the hotel's history, she wanted to know it. "Please, tell me all about Ernest."

Tom was quick to take the lead. "It was a dark and stormy night," he began with dramatic flair.

"It was?" interrupted Julie. "I don't remember that."

"Would you prefer to tell the story?" Tom asked his wife with a hint of annoyance.

"No, go ahead," Julie replied crossly.

Tom regained his theatrical pose. "The year was 1864. Ernest was both a God-fearing preacher and a hard-working cowboy. He had spent his life teaching the benefits of being good and true. He and his brother were driving a herd of cattle westward across Arizona with their wives and children on their way to relocate to California. A storm stopped them early that fateful day. They set up camp on this very property. It had seemed like a hospitable place to wait out the storm. But little did they know that a band of local thieves had set up camp nearby."

Tom inhaled a melodramatic breath before continuing. "The band of thieves set their sights on the temporary encampment of Ernest's family. The wicked thieves crept towards the canvas tent as the wind howled and rain poured down on them. Ernest was leading the family in their evening prayers before bedtime as they did every night. With the noise of the storm, there was no way that any of them could have known they were about to be attacked. And yet, Ernest suddenly knew. A divine inspiration and awareness took hold of him. He walked out of the tent with a fearlessness he had never before experienced. In his hand he held his family's only weapon: an old rifle.

"Ernest came upon the rag tag group of dirty thieves and stood in front of the tent, protecting his family. As the four thieves inched closer, Ernest raised his rifle and aimed. He hoped the thieves would be frightened enough to run away. Ernest had spent his life teaching and believing the commandment *Thou Shalt Not Kill*. He did not want to break a commandment. Three of the thieves stopped their advance, but the youngest of them was also the meanest, and he kept coming at Ernest. Ernest could not find it in his good nature to shoot the young man. The youth grabbed the gun and the two men struggled. Finally, the strength of youth won out and the thief aimed the rifle at Ernest and shot him point blank. Ernest hit the ground, dead.

"The other thieves were horrified. They were thieves, not murderers. They forcefully grabbed their young murderous companion and ran, leaving Ernest's rifle by his side.

"Ernest's family buried him right there on that very spot that night. They buried the rifle with him, never wanting to look at the weapon that killed their beloved husband, father, brother, and uncle.

"His family thought they had laid him to rest that night, but Ernest never truly began to rest. In life, Ernest protected his family that night. In death, Ernest vowed to protect all the good people of this property for eternity. He has spent his afterlife championing those who are kind and good and wreaking vengeance on those who are mean and wicked.

"So, when you hear an unexplained noise or see something out of the corner of your eye, that is Ernest. When this happens, you must ask yourself 'Am I being good or am I being bad?' This will determine your fate with Ernest, the guardian of the ranch."

Millicent started clapping. "Very nice. You have quite the memory, Tom," she said.

After Tom's ghost story, there was a lull in conversation during which Eve desperately wanted to bring up the subject of Dirk's death, but she determined it would be uncouth. Instead, she said "There isn't anything scheduled tomorrow morning so you can all do what you want. Please feel free to use the pool or go exploring around the property. Wes will be available at the stables, if anyone would like to go horseback riding again. But, please take plenty of water and wear a sun hat."

"A sun hat? It's about to start storming out there," said Ben. The end of his sentence was punctuated by a comically timed clap of thunder that made everyone jump. "See?" he said as everyone chuckled.

Suddenly, the sound of pouring rain surrounded the hotel.

"Yes, as Ben— and nature— just pointed out, it is monsoon season," said Eve, "but our rain usually comes in the afternoon or evenings. The mornings tend to be bright and hot."

"Well, I know what I want to do tomorrow morning," Gil said shiftily.

"What?" Eve asked.

"I want to go out to the shooting range and pick up those rusty cans for you."

"No, I told you—" Eve stopped. She realized that this subject allowed her to bring up Dirk organically, so she jumped at the chance. "Hey, that reminds me— the shooting range closed in 1977, right? You guys had to close it down because of Dirk's death, right?"

"Yes," Gil said cautiously as he took a sip of beer.

"So, who killed him?" Eve asked.

Gil slowly opened his mouth, but Millicent spoke first. "She knows it wasn't a guest."

"So, it had to be someone who worked here," Eve pointed out. "But you never found out who it was?" she asked the group.

"No one knew and no one cared enough about Dirk to find out," said Tom.

"Our biggest concern was keeping it from Mr. Thorton," said Walter loudly, directly, with no signs of confusion. Everyone was shocked. Walter had been seemingly in another world and silent all night. His sudden shrewdness was a surprise to everyone. He continued by saying, "It was of the utmost importance to maintain the reputation of the hotel and the ranch. Everyone understood that."

They all waited for Walter to say something else, but although his eyes were still clear with comprehension, he remained silent.

"It sounded like no one cared for the man," prompted Eve.

During the ensuing moment of awkward silence, the rain became harder and louder. It filled the room with the noise that Eve always joked was the sound of impending doom. Eve looked enquiringly at Gil. She thought she could rely on Gil's affable nature to instinctively keep the conversation flowing. It worked.

Gil said, "Well, I didn't know him that well, myself, but he seemed off. He was a little creepy, I thought."

"What do you mean?" Eve prodded.

"I just remember this one time…" Gil began. "Well, we all used to always talk about how cute Annabelle was."

"Why thank you," Annabelle cut in as she comically smoothed her hair.

Gil smiled at her and continued. "She was the only kid around here and she was really adorable and sweet natured. Everyone loved her. So, like I said, we all talked about how cute she was all the time. But when I heard Dirk say she was cute, it just creeped me out. I can't explain it really. And he was always trying to kill rabbits and squirrels. I mean, I hunt, I kill animals for food. But he just wanted to kill things for fun. But, like I said, I didn't really know him. He just gave me the creeps and I didn't want to get to know him, so I didn't."

Tom had a sour look on his face as he said, "He was definitely a creep, he —,"

"Sterling," Julie interrupted. "Didn't Dirk borrow a bunch of money from you and never paid it back?"

"Yes," Sterling answered simply.

"He stole from you too?" asked Millicent. "He was a no-good thief and liar. A cretin, through and through," she said with finality.

It was Ben's turn to press for information. "So, this guy was murdered by one of you?"

"No!" said Sterling and Tom in unison.

"I didn't mean one of you sitting here, I meant one of

the people that worked here back then."

"I'm sure it was an accident," Julie told her son.

"But—" Ben began but was cut off by his mother repeating herself.

"I'm sure it was an accident," she said more forcefully. Julie gave Ben a stern motherly stare that said *Shut Your Mouth.*

Defeated, Ben said, "I'm going to bed."

"Me too," said Gil. "That last beer put me over the edge of tired."

Ben and Gil walked up the steps together. When they got to the balcony, Ben conspiratorially asked Gil, "It was murder, right?"

Just before entering his room, Gil said, "Oh, yeah, definitely murder. And I know who did it."

Just then, another thunderclap shook the building. Everyone jumped again. But this time there was no accompanying laughter. Little did Ben and Gil know that their seemingly private conversation upstairs had echoed perfectly down below for everyone to hear. The group in the lobby had been shocked into an unnerving silence.

Chapter Fourteen

The Friday morning shone bright and clean from last night's storm. As Eve leisurely stretched her arms and sat up in bed, she tried to remember what she had learned last night before falling asleep. For her bedtime reading she had chosen to research the Sandmat Sentinel archives for her mentions of her current guests.

She remembered that she had first tried Walter Flint with no results.

She then searched for Annabelle Sheridan. When it revealed no search results, she remembered that she needed to type Annabelle Flint. After she did that, she got a hit. She found a picture with a caption from a May 1977 newspaper. The caption read; *Miss Annabelle Flint wins the Juniper County Sheriff's Shooting Competition for the second year in a row.* The picture featured young Annabelle holding up a trophy while the sheriff shook hands with Walter. All three of them were smiling jovially.

Then she had searched for Tom Hayward but found nothing. She hadn't been able to remember Julie's maiden name and she didn't know Sterling's first name so she had skipped them.

When she had searched for Gil Dancer, a shocking number of search results popped up. As Eve randomly selected a few of the entries, she realized most of the articles mentioned Gil because he had been on the Sandmat Chamber of Commerce for many years. Then she found an interesting article when Gil opened Dancer Diner. It featured a picture showing him in front of the new building cutting a ribbon, surrounded by unnamed townspeople. She looked at the happy faces wondering why the woman standing next to Gil wasn't smiling. Then she realized that was the woman's normal look of disapproval. It was Millicent. At first Eve thought it was odd that Millicent was there, but then asked herself, *why would it be*? Millicent had been Gil's culinary mentor and she lived in the area. Certainly, he would invite her to the opening of his restaurant.

Daisy Malone had not resulted in any hits, nor had Millicent. Eve got up and looked out the window at the bright, beautiful day with a nagging thought in the back of her brain that something was wrong. She ignored it and thought about how sad it was that Millicent had lived in the area for over thirty years, yet there was no mention of her in the archives. It was like she never existed. Eve hoped that she would make her mark and someday have her name in the Sentinel archives like Gil. Of course, she was a business owner like Gil, so she would likely be in the paper for that. Especially, since she was having her grand opening soon.

Oh no! Eve ran her fingers through her slightly matted hair. She had forgotten to invite the press to her grand opening! What an unforgiveable oversight! Of course, in this rural area, the press was really just a guy named Slim. In Juniper County, to alert the local media to an event was as simple as telling someone who knew Slim to tell him to show up somewhere. But she had forgotten to do even that! She hoped Slim wasn't otherwise engaged that day. She would see if Gil could make the arrangements for her.

If not, Eve could just prepare her own press release and send it to the Sandmat Sentinel. With as little staff as they had, they would probably appreciate being sent a pre-written article and a picture, and then she could make sure she made her debut in the local news. *Yes, that's the ticket,* Eve said to herself in her internal 1940s newspaper reporter voice. *I'm gonna be a star, baby!*

Eve was laughing to herself when it finally hit her what was wrong with the bright, beautiful day: it was too bright! The sun was high in sky already which meant that it was not early. As a lifelong light sleeper and early riser, Eve was not in the habit of needing an alarm clock. But she should have used one this morning. She was horrified to realize that it was after 9:00 am. She quickly got ready and rushed out to the lobby to find no one there. She peeked into the dining room and again found no one. She hurried into the kitchen and found Esperanza and Ramon cleaning up breakfast dishes.

"There you are!" said Esperanza. "We were getting worried."

"I'm so sorry. I guess I'm getting more and more comfortable here and sleeping better. And I think I've been relying on Sunset jumping on me in the morning to get up early. Tomorrow, I'll set my alarm. I'm so embarrassed."

"No need. I do not want to give you the impression that your absence was not noticed or that your presence was not missed," said Ramon, "but rest assured, the morning's events went smoothly. You have an incredibly capable staff."

"I guess I have to if I'm going to be a loser who sleeps in. I'm really horrified. But thank you so much for being amazing."

"Of course!" said Esperanza wearing a grin. "But you're not a loser, you're just human and humans need sleep."

"So, where is everybody?" Eve asked.

"Loretta and Roxie are tidying up the rooms," said Esperanza. "I think some of the guests went to the pool and some went for another horseback ride. They said they didn't need Wes's help, so Wes went out with Gil to the old shooting range to pick up those rusty cans."

"What? I told him he didn't need to do that!" said Eve. "Great, not only do I sleep in but now one of my guests is doing work that I was too lazy to do! I have a desperate need to be productive. How can I help you?"

"We are just about done with cleanup, but we need help with the preparations for the barbecue this afternoon," said Esperanza. "I have a mountain of potatoes that need to be diced up for potato salad."

"Perfect! That sounds like something I can handle. Just show me exactly how you want it done."

As Eve was finishing her potato project, Loretta and Roxie walked into the kitchen.

"Okay, we're done with the rooms. What can we do?" asked Loretta.

Eve noticed that Roxie's face was bright red, and she was avoiding looking at anyone. Roxie was obviously embarrassed about something. Eve was always surprised at the little things that would embarrass Roxie. And yet at other times, when Eve thought Roxie should be embarrassed, she wasn't.

"Now that you have reinforcements, I think I'm going to abandon you," Eve said to Esperanza and Ramon. "I just can't help but feel guilty about Gil being out there picking up those rusty cans. I feel like I need to go out and help. And bring them some water or iced tea."

"That is a great idea," said Ramon. "Gil is a fanatic about iced tea, and I just made some." Ramon opened the walk-in refrigerator and grabbed a sealed pitcher of iced tea. "Here, you can take this one."

Esperanza grabbed the pitcher, put it in a basket with some glasses wrapped in a towel and handed it to Eve.

"Thank you. Thank you for everything, all of you."

She left her staff to continue with the extensive food preparation for the barbecue.

While still chastising herself for sleeping in, she unconsciously made a mental note of her mileage as she put on her seatbelt. On her drive out to the old shooting range, she vowed to herself that she would be better, she would focus all her efforts on being a good hostess to her very first hotel guests.

She pulled into the parking area that was hidden from the shooting range by a cluster of short, fat pinion pine trees. She parked next to Gil's old pickup truck. In the back of her mind something about his truck registered as different. But she didn't dwell on it since she was focused on deciding whether she would thank or admonish Gil for picking up the rusty cans. She supposed, as a good hostess, one shouldn't lecture or yell at one's guests. She would thank him.

She opened the back door to retrieve the basket of iced tea when a loud sharp noise scared her enough to make her jump. *Was that a gunshot?* thought Eve as she instinctually crouched down. Her heart was racing. She stayed still and waited, but only silence followed. As she began to calm herself, she stared at Gil's pickup truck. She now realized what was different: one of the guns in his gun rack was missing.

Her obsession with being a good hostess completely abandoned her. She was mad that Gil and Wes were using the shooting range when she had expressly asked for no shooting on her property. They had just scared her and she was mad. She left the iced tea in the back of the car, slammed the door shut, and marched along the path that led to the old shooting range along the hillside.

As she got closer to Gil and Wes and tried to make sense of the scene in front of her, her anger lessened as her worry increased. Wes was sitting on the ground and Gil was kneeling beside him. She looked for Gil's gun but saw only work gloves and a trash bag on the ground.

When it finally occurred to her that Gil was tending to an injured Wes, her panic propelled her to run to them.

"What happened? Are you okay?" She asked frantically.

Wes looked up at her and said, "Yep. Fine… Fine… Yep, Fine."

Eve decided he must be in shock. She looked to Gil for answers.

"He's okay, just a scratch," Gil said.

Eve finally saw the mark on Wes's upper arm. "Is that a bullet wound?"

Gil calmly said, "Well… yes, but really, he's fine."

Eve knelt down by Wes and looked at the injury.

Gil walked away and made a phone call.

"What happened?" Eve asked Wes.

"I don't know," Wes said dreamily.

"Were you guys out here shooting? Did Gil accidentally shoot you?"

The questions seemed to help Wes come out of his daze. "No, we weren't shooting," he said. "We were just picking up cans. Then I heard a shot and felt a pain in my arm. I tripped on a rock and fell down. I think I'm okay. Yep, I'm fine. Really. I'm fine."

Although Eve agreed that the wound was far from life threatening, she said, "No macho stupidity on my watch. You're going to the hospital. I'm not going to let you walk off a bullet wound."

Eve helped Wes off the ground. Gil ended the phone call and walked back to them.

"Did the 911 dispatcher say how long an ambulance will be?" Eve asked.

"Well, no, but you could be halfway to the hospital by the time one gets here. You should just drive him," suggested Gil as the trio began the walk back to their vehicles.

They walked in contemplative silence. When they arrived at the parking area, Eve said, "I think you should drive him, Gil."

"Your brand-new SUV can make it there a lot faster than my old truck," he countered.

"But I want you to get out of here, Gil." Eve stared at him intently as she said, "I think someone just tried to kill you."

Chapter Fifteen

Gil finally conceded to Eve's wish that he be the one to take Wes to the hospital in her SUV. She promised Gil that she would drive his truck back to the hotel immediately. She watched Gil drive away with Wes as her thoughts ran wild. Even though she wanted to get out of there as fast as possible, she decided to make a phone call first.

It wasn't until she was halfway back that it occurred to her that she may have put herself in danger. If there was someone out there trying to shoot Gil, driving his truck might be incredibly unwise. She anxiously listened for gunfire the entire drive back to the hotel.

When she arrived at the hotel parking lot, she was ecstatic to see the calvary she had called was making its way up the driveway. As soon as she exited Gil's truck, Sheriff Strider pulled up and parked his Juniper County Sheriff's Department SUV next to her. She quickly opened the passenger door and got in the SUV. He gave her a perplexed look.

After Eve closed the door, she said, "It feels safe in here. I feel like I can't get shot in a cop car."

"I don't think you understand how much more likely you are to get shot at in a law enforcement vehicle."

She laughed nervously.

"I'm glad I was in the area when you called. What exactly is going on?"

She told him what happened and mentioned the missing gun in Gil's truck.

"Are you sure it wasn't an accident? It is the old shooting range, right?"

"I expressly asked that no one shoot on the property. Gil and Wes were obviously picking up cans. I don't see how it could possibly be an accident. I also don't think the shooting in 1977 was an accident either."

"1977?"

Eve proceeded to tell Strider about the forty-six year old death at the shooting range and Gil's concerning statement the night before.

"The more I heard yesterday," she continued, "the more I became certain that Dirk was murdered, but I thought he was probably shot by one of the other ranch hands." She took a deep breath before she said, "but now I think that Dirk was killed by someone here."

Strider drove Eve back out to the shooting range so she could show him the scene of the crime. When they drove by the employee cabins, she noticed that Millicent's car was parked there. Thinking back, she realized that she had seen it there on the way out to bring the iced tea but she hadn't thought anything about seeing a vehicle in that parking area. On the way back to the hotel after the shooting, she had other things on her mind like hoping she wasn't going to be shot at, but now she noted it as strange. From the cabins it wasn't too long of a walk to the old shooting range.

When they arrived at the shooting range, she showed Strider where Wes was shot and pointed out the grove of trees that she assumed the shooter had been hiding in. Strider looked around the mess of rusty cans and then asked her to wait while he searched the grove of juniper trees. As he walked out of the grove he was on his phone. He hung up before he arrived back at the vehicle.

On their drive back toward the hotel, Sheriff Strider asked, "So, how do you want to play this?"

"Me? Aren't you in charge?"

"I'm not here officially."

"You're not?"

"You called my personal number. There wasn't a 911 call dispatched to the sheriff's office. And it seems like — "

"Pull over!" ordered Eve. "Please." She pointed to what had caught her eye: Millicent walking towards her car in the cabin parking area.

Strider slowed and parked his SUV next to Millicent's car. Eve jumped out of the car before it was completely stopped.

As Eve approached Millicent, she noted her red eyes and tear-stained face.

"Are you okay?" Eve asked.

"Yes. I'm fine." Despite a noticeable determination to appear composed, Millicent's attempt to hide her recent crying was unsuccessful. But Millicent's hardened countenance told Eve she was not interested in discussing it.

"Did you hear a gunshot earlier?" Eve asked.

"Maybe. I suppose so. I didn't think much of it," Millicent said as her eyes moved to watch Sheriff Strider exiting his vehicle.

"Why are you out here?" Eve asked.

"Am I not allowed to be out here?" Millicent asked defensively while her eyes remained on Strider. "Am I trespassing?" She looked back at Eve with a bitter stare and said, "Are you having me arrested?"

"No, of course not," Eve said hurriedly. She quickly explained the situation making sure to tell her that Gil had taken Wes to the hospital.

"Oh, thank God the boy's not hurt," Millicent said with compassion before her resting look of contempt once again took hold. "It was probably that idiot boy of Tom and Julie's. He kept talking about guns and shooting yesterday. He was probably screwing around and now look what he's done." She looked at Sheriff Strider and said, "You should throw him in your cells for a night and teach him a lesson."

Before Eve or Strider could say anything else, Millicent jumped into her car and sped off toward the hotel. Eve couldn't help but notice that, for 78, Millicent was very quick on her feet.

"So..." Sheriff Strider said to snap Eve out of her reverie.

"Yeah," she said as she turned her attention back to him. "You were saying something about it seeming like..."

"My gut says that this was an accident. One shot and one miss doesn't sound like a murderous rampage."

"The shooter probably got scared because they hit the wrong guy! That doesn't mean that they won't try again if Gil was the intended target. I'm sure this has something to do with Dirk's murder."

"Didn't you tell me that even Gil thinks it was an accident?"

"Yes, he said he thought it was just someone playing around, but of course he doesn't want to think that someone is trying to murder him."

"Do you think that maybe you are overreacting because of your recent murder related trauma?"

Eve gave the sheriff such a pointedly hateful stare he cowered and said, "Okay, I'm sorry. So, back to my original question... How do you want to play this? It's your call."

"I want to find out what happened. I'm not going to ignore the fact that someone almost killed Wes, or Gil. So, I would like to question everybody about their whereabouts during the shooting. And... it might be kind of nice to have a sheriff standing next to me while I do that to encourage honest answers."

"That can work in your favor with some people but for others the presence of law enforcement breeds the instinct to keep quiet or lie."

"I'll take my chances with you." Eve felt her face become uncomfortably warm. "I mean I'll take my chances with having law enforcement present... Let's go," she said quickly as she got back into the car.

Chapter Sixteen

Strider parked on the circle drive right in front of the hotel. Before they exited the car, Eve turned to Strider.

"Yes, maybe I am letting my imagination get away from me. Maybe I do have some unresolved issues about murder. Maybe this was an accident. But I need to know. So, thank you for coming. It was very reassuring having my own personal calvary arrive when I was so flustered."

"You are always very welcome," Sheriff Strider said kindly. He then reminded her that he was not there officially, she would have to do all the talking. He suggested some interviewing tactics and asked her to give him a run down of the guests again. After she gave him all the details of each guest, they exited the vehicle.

Eve was ready to start uncovering the truth. As she walked up the porch steps she took a deep breath and mentally prepared herself to set aside her role as amenable hostess to play the part of hardened detective.

As soon as the serious couple walked into the lobby they were greeted by Loretta and a suspiciously smiling Roxie.

"What were you doing in the car for so long?" asked

Roxie. "Were you guys out there throating?"

Eve and Strider stared at her with confusion.

"Not 'throating'! It's 'necking', Roxanne, 'necking'," Loretta corrected her daughter. Loretta then turned to the sheriff and her boss, her face bright red with shame. "Sorry! Last night, we was watching an old movie and she got obsessed with the words she never heard before." Loretta grabbed Roxie by the arm and marched her into the kitchen.

Eve's tough detective persona had evaporated with the minor humiliation. Intent on trying to hide her embarrassment, she refused to look at Strider. Instead, she searched the hotel for any of her guests.

Her plan had been to question each person separately, revealing Wes's shooting to them to see the look on each face when they heard the news. All her hopes were dashed. She saw that the entire group, save Ben, was on the veranda surrounding Millicent, who was waving her arms as if regaling a most interesting story.

Eve took in the scene, taking advantage of the fact that the group outside in the bright sun was unaware that they were being watched by Eve and Strider in the dark lobby.

Julie had one of the bright orange pool towels (that Eve had proudly picked out to complement the turquoise pool furniture) draped over a large tote bag. In the other hand she held a pink stainless-steel water bottle. Her hair was wet, it appeared she had just come from the pool.

Sterling was wearing his big boonie sun hat and carrying his ever-present canvas duffel bag. Daisy was wearing a big floppy hat and was covered in a sea of gauzy clothing.

Walter and Annabelle looked like they had been in the sun for too long. They were both wearing head-to-toe dark colors, Annabelle in all black and Walter in dark blues. They were not wearing hats or carrying any bags, or bottles of water. Eve's inner mother hen was annoyed. She told everyone to always take water if they went out exploring. Annabelle should especially make sure her father kept hydrated in the summer heat.

Tom was holding a straw cowboy hat in his hand, the one he wore riding yesterday, and he was wearing his cowboy boots. She was contented to see he had a water bottle that matched Julie's, but in green. Eve assumed he must have gone on a horseback ride. The the tell-tale sign of dark horsehair on his light blue jeans confirmed it. As the group talked, Tom took turns looking at Julie and looking out towards the direction of the shooting range.

Sterling broke away from the group and came inside. He entered the lobby, saw Eve and the sheriff and silently nodded a wooden greeting.

"I can take your bag up for you if you'd like," Eve said artlessly. She desperately wanted to see if there was a rifle in that bag. But since she had a sheriff next to her, her pretense of simply playing hostess wasn't working.

Sterling pulled his bag a little closer and said, "No thank you, I've got it." His long legs took the steps two at a time, and he was in his room in the blink of an eye.

"That was suspicious," said Strider.

"Maybe. He's a naturally guarded and quiet man," responded Eve. "Let's go talk to the rest of them."

Strider obediently followed her through the dining room and out onto the veranda. As they arrived and the group caught sight of the sheriff everyone seemed to tense up. The air of agitation turned into defensiveness. Perhaps having law enforcement here wasn't the best idea. Oh, well, it was happening this way, she may as well jump in.

Tom had been about to make a phone call and put away his phone as he eyed Sheriff Strider.

"I assume that you all know about Wes getting shot," said Eve as she surveyed the small crowd.

Heads nodded and Annabelle said, "He's alright though. Right? That's what... what Millie said, that he wasn't hurt badly. Right?" She looked at Eve anxiously.

"Yes, he is fine, thankfully," Eve replied. "But he or Gil could have easily been killed. I specifically asked that there be no shooting on the property. Do any of you know what happened?"

Silent heads shook.

"Did you hear the gunshot?" Eve asked the group, but then thought she should ask the question individually. "Annabelle, did you hear the gunshot?"

"Yes. Dad and I were taking a walk when we heard it. I wasn't sure where it had come from, but it concerned me, so we turned back and returned to the hotel."

"And you, Daisy? Did you hear it?"

"Me? I don't know."

"Where were you?"

"Where was I? I was… I was out at the vineyard. I've always loved walking around the vineyard. So quiet, so peaceful, so restorative."

Eve noticed that Tom shot Daisy a strange, puzzled look. Daisy did not seem to notice.

"What about you, Tom. Did you hear it?"

"Sure."

"Where were you?"

"I had gone out on a ride with Sterling."

"So, you were together?"

"We were, but we separated. We wanted to go in different directions. I was out on the other side of the property heading back to the stables when I heard the gunshot."

"What horses did you take out?" Eve asked.

"I rode Maverick, and Sterling was on the Appaloosa. Gertie, I think her name is."

"What about you Julie?" Eve asked. "Where were you when you heard the gunshot?"

"I didn't hear anything."

"You didn't?"

"No. I was at the swimming pool all morning. I can only assume I was underwater at the time."

"And what about Ben?" Eve asked Julie.

Julie shot Tom a quick look before saying, "I'm sure he's been in his room all morning. He's not overly fond of the outdoors."

"And where were you when you heard the gun shot, Millicent?"

"I was at the cabins. You already know that," she said to Eve while giving Sheriff Strider a suspicious stare.

"Where were you, exactly?" Eve asked uncompromisingly. She needed to show Millicent that she too could be tough when needed.

"I was looking in the window of the bunkhouse." Millicent's demeanor suddenly softened. "If you must know, I was reminiscing about some of those young cowboys that worked here over the years. A lot of those boys were like sons to me and Buck." Millicent blinked back a tear as she looked at Annabelle and said, "And Annabelle was like a daughter to us."

Annabelle burst into tears so suddenly and violently that it startled Eve.

"Oh, Millie," said Annabelle once she had composed herself a little. "You were like a second mother to me. I'm so sorry we lost touch." Annabelle approached a wooden and reluctant Millicent and gave her a hug. After a moment, Millicent relaxed and hugged her back.

Eve was torn. The hostess in her was touched at the emotional scene and overjoyed that her reunion was such a success. In her role as amateur detective, she was annoyed that her group interrogation had deteriorated into a sappy mess worthy of a soap opera. She became even more vexed when she saw that Sheriff Strider was trying to keep a straight face. Apparently, he was amused by the antics of daytime television.

Strider's phone rang. He answered it and walked away down the path towards the pool for privacy. With the sheriff's absence, the group took the opportunity to quickly disperse.

"Dad, let's get you some water," said Annabelle as she guided her father towards the door to the dining room. Millicent followed them inside.

Tom walked off to the horse pasture fence and made a phone call. Julie watched her husband until she realized that Eve was watching her. Julie quickly said, "I'm going to go take a shower." Then, clutching her large tote bag and pool towel she hurried inside.

Eve stood on the veranda watching Tom on the phone, unable to hear his conversation and feeling useless as a detective. She looked down the path. Strider was walking back, all amusement wiped from his face.

"I have to go," he said seriously. "There's a rollover automobile accident on 66 towards Sandmat. Are you okay?"

"Yes, I'm fine. Go."

"Okay," he said hurriedly as he started to walk off. "Call me if you need anything."

All of a sudden, Eve realized that she hadn't yet told her staff about Wes. She should do that before they heard the news from someone else. Eve walked into the dining room as Annabelle and Walter were about to leave.

"I think my dad needs a nap. Maybe I do too," said Annabelle.

"Did you go for a ride this morning?" Eve asked Annabelle as she looked at the light-colored horsehair on Annabelle's dark pants.

"No, I was just walking with Dad all morning." Annabelle looked down at the horsehair. "Must have been from yesterday."

"I know. Between the horses and my dog, I seem to always be wearing animal hair." Eve attempted a smile and headed towards the kitchen. She missed her dog. Seeing him would make her feel so much better right now. But she was glad he wasn't here. If someone was carelessly shooting on her property, she would certainly not want him running around. She shivered at the idea of

Sunset being in harm's way.

Chapter Seventeen

Esperanza, Ramon, Loretta, and Roxie were in the kitchen, serenely preparing food, and listening to music. She hated to ruin the pleasant moment, but she did. She told them what happened, assured them that Wes was fine, and answered all their questions. They had no idea anything had happened. They told her that they had all been in the kitchen preparing food while taking turns getting to choose what music they listened to. They hadn't heard a gunshot.

Eve decided to unburden herself of all her thoughts. She confided in them the story of Dirk's murder, Gil's comment that he knew who did it, and her suspicion that the 1977 murder and the shooting this morning might be connected.

"And anyone could have done it!" Eve vented. "I gave everyone time to return to the hotel." She was annoyed with herself when she realized that. "And no one has an alibi. Everyone, save Annabelle who was with her dad, everyone was alone."

"Annabelle's the blonde lady?" Loretta asked.

"Yes," replied Eve.

"I seen her when I was sweeping the balcony of Suite A," Loretta said. "She was walking but I'm pretty sure she was alone."

"Everyone keeps telling me that they are sure it was an accident and not to worry about it," Eve said as she ran her fingers through her hair. She then admitted to her staff that she didn't know what to do now. Should she let it go or try to figure out what happened?

"You let something go? Ha!" Loretta said.

Roxie laughed. "Yeah, Eve. I don't see that happening. You better figure it out or you'll go crazy."

"I would certainly like to know who shot Wes," said Esperanza. "And it better have been an accident, or they are going to have to deal with me," she said with a maternal fierceness.

"I have a suggestion, if you do not mind," said Ramon.

"Please," said a distraught Eve.

"On your schedule of events, you have more history interviews to conduct, correct?"

"Yes."

"Perhaps you can appear to let the matter lie and move on with your schedule, but use those interviews to casually ask questions that might reveal some answers about what happened today."

"Okay," Eve said as her mental wheels started moving a little bit faster, "that might work. But I need to also talk to one person I wasn't planning on interviewing." A determined Eve walked out of the room without explaining.

As the swing door closed behind her, she stopped in surprise. Standing in the middle of the lobby was the person she was about to search for.

"Ben. There you are. Can I talk to you in my office?" She motioned for him to follow her.

As she closed the office door behind Ben, he said with a smirk, "Am I in trouble? I feel like I just got sent to the principal's office."

"This isn't funny, Ben. Wes was shot," she said bluntly.

"I heard. He's not dead or hurt bad or anything."

"He could have been killed! He or Gil could have been killed."

"Gil was out there too?"

Eve couldn't tell if he was pretending his ignorance. "You know, Ben, when Gil and you were up on the balcony last night and he told you that he knew Dirk was murdered and he knew who did it— everyone downstairs heard that."

"You did?"

"Yes. Do you know anything about the shooting this morning?"

"No."

"I need to know if it was an accident or if it was intentional. I need to know if someone was trying to hurt Gil."

"Why would anyone try and hurt Gil?"

"Because of what he said to you last night. That he knew who killed Dirk."

"Oh, I see," he said with his mouth but not his eyes.

"Did you hear the gunshot?"

"No."

"Where were you this morning?"

"In my room gaming. I had my headphones on," explained Ben. "I didn't hear nothing," he added defensively.

"Did anyone see you this morning?"

"Like, do I have an alibi? Um, no. I was in my room by myself."

"You were the one who was talking about shooting. Some people think that it was probably you."

"Me? No way! How about the crazy old man or the mean old witch, or the super loony lady. I mean, come on, take your pick. Or even better, how about the scary sniper dude?"

"Sniper dude?"

"Yeah." Ben looked at Eve as if she were stupid. "The guy with the scar on his face. The one that looks like the poster boy for PTSD."

"What are you talking about Ben?"

"That guy, Sterling. On the drive over here, my parents were talking about the people who were going to be here. They were talking about how Sterling joined the army after leaving the hotel. They heard he was a sniper. And he looks like a killer to me," he concluded as he resolutely crossed his arms.

Eve was not impressed by Ben's closing argument. She let him go. She wasn't sure if she believed anything he said. Of all the people in the hotel, she trusted him the least, well maybe second to least after Daisy's arrival. But Daisy was kooky whereas Ben had already proven himself to be a liar. Eve also didn't care for the way he was a little too eager to pin the blame on everyone else. And, on top of it, yet again, Ben chose to wear the most inappropriate T-shirt for the situation. This time it had read "In my defense, I was left unsupervised."

She felt riled and useless. She looked down at her schedule of events. She was supposed to be having her interview with Sterling right now. She decided to take Ramon's advice. She went upstairs and knocked on Sterling's door.

"Hello," Eve said perhaps too cheerily when the door opened. "Are you ready for your history interview about your job and life here at the Arizona Sunset Ranch Hotel?"

"Uh… yeah, sure," Sterling said before he grabbed his duffel bag. "Downstairs?"

"Yes, in my office." Eve tried to shake off her feeling of discomfort and worry as she walked down the stairs, through the lobby, and finally into the office with the intimidating man carrying a duffel bag big enough to carry a rifle, or worse. Who knew what he carried around in there?

Once they were settled into the office chairs, Eve steeled herself and said, "Before we get started, I'd like to know where you were this morning when you heard the gunshot."

"I didn't."

"Weren't you out horseback riding this morning?"

"Yes."

"Then you should have heard it."

"I must have been too far away, either physically or mentally. Sometimes when I get really focused on something, I don't know what's going on around me."

"And you were really focused on something?"

"Yes. I'm a birder," said Sterling, as if that was the explanation to every question Eve could possibly have.

"A burber?"

"A birder," Sterling corrected her with a hint of a smile. "A bird watcher."

"Oh."

"I know it sounds strange to non-birders, but we get engrossed in our endeavors. A bit obsessive, really."

"Oh," Eve said again. She was taken aback by this insight into Sterling's personality.

"Here, I'll show you." Sterling leaned over and unzipped his duffel bag that lay on the floor by his side.

Eve held her breath and craned her neck so that she could see inside the open bag. Sterling removed a large black plastic case revealing underneath a tripod, a scope, and binoculars. He opened the case he had removed and pulled out a professional looking camera with a long lens.

As he turned his camera on to review the pictures that he had taken this morning, he said, "I was spending some quality time with a Red-Naped Sapsucker."

"That sounds like a monster from a horror movie," Eve said, intrigued.

The corner of Sterling's mouth twitched up with a slight smile. "It's a woodpecker. Perhaps I was too engrossed in its pecking noises to register the sound of anything else. Here's a picture of him." He turned the camera to show Eve a gorgeous picture of a stunning black and white woodpecker with a yellow belly and a beautifully bright red head.

"Wow, he is a head-turner," Eve said with surprise. "And I have that on my property?"

"Yes," Sterling said as he continued to sift through his digital photos. "I noticed you have bird feeders around the property. You must have some interest in birds."

"I like them, but honestly, I don't know anything about them. As far as telling them apart, I know I have little brown ones and bigger brown ones. That's about it," she said with a laugh. "And the hummingbirds, of course. Oh, and then I have my land birds: my quail and my roadrunners. I love those guys."

"So, you know most of your locals. Your brown birds are probably house finches, and house sparrows. And you may want to keep an eye out on your cliff back," he said as he nodded towards the north side of the property. "I think you might have some golden eagles nesting up there. By this time of the year, the eaglets will be matured and just out of the nest. I want to get a closer look tomorrow."

"Really? Fantastic! Oh, I did also see a flock of bluebirds the other day. I guess they were bluebirds, being both blue and birds. I didn't notice at first but then they all swooped by and when their backs faced the sunlight, the blue was so bright. It was gorgeous!"

"Yes. Western Bluebirds. I was lucky enough to see some of those beauties yesterday."

"I called them a flock," said Eve. "Are a group of them called a flock? Or are they called something strange? You know, like a group of crows is called a murder. Oh, and owls... What are a bunch of owls called? It's something cool..."

"A parliament," Sterling replied.

"Yes, a parliament of owls. I love that!"

"You were correct in using the term flock. Ornithologists— both birders and scientists do not use those terms. They are archaic and just a bit of fun trivia." He pointed the camera's viewing screen at Eve once again. "Here is an industrious little Lesser Goldfinch I met with this morning also."

As Eve admired the fluffy yellow bird, she wondered if Sterling was taking advantage of her natural thirst for knowledge to distract her from her inquiry into this morning's incident. If so, he was good. She had almost completely forgotten her goal. She banished the thought of birds from her mind and changed tacks.

"Can I ask you a non-bird related question?" She quickly interjected before he distracted her with yet another adorable bird.

"Sure," he responded affably.

"Who murdered Dirk?"

His countenance turned gloomy. "I don't know. And to be honest, I'm not sure that I care. And for the record, I don't think Gil ever knew either. I know we all heard him say that stupid comment last night, but I think he was just being dramatic, telling tall tales. People who actually have dramatic tales to tell keep them to themselves."

"Did you know Dirk?"

"There are a lot of people I have known over the years whose memories deserve to be kept alive. Dirk is not one of those people. I suggest you forget about him."

Sterling the joyful birder had vanished. The intimidating man with the scary scar on his face had returned. But Eve had one more question to ask.

"Who do you think shot Wes this morning?"

Eve noticed the slightest change in his demeanor as he said, "I'm sure it was an accident. We should all just be thankful no one was seriously hurt."

Eve stared at Sterling suspiciously. She couldn't make this guy out. He was a bit strange, but was he a harmless eccentric or was he unstable?

"You can't suspect me," he said bluntly. "First of all, I have incredibly safe gun handling habits. Secondly, I am a great shot. The only way I would have winged your horse wrangler was if that was my intention. And why, I ask you, would I want to do that?"

Eve certainly had no response to that question. But the fact that it was a rhetorical question did not preclude it from having an answer. Eve herself was skilled at the art of not lying without telling the truth. She got the impression that Sterling was also.

"And one of the reasons I am a good shot," Sterling continued with an easier air, "is because of my days as a young man as the gardener and shooting range guide here at the Arizona Sunset Ranch Hotel."

Eve accepted Sterling's transition to the history interview and turned on her recording app. After all, she still wanted to learn about the past workings of the hotel.

Chapter Eighteen

Eve's mind was bouncing from one subject to another as she sat in one of the large red rocking chairs on the front porch of the hotel, staring out west at old U.S. Highway 66, now Historic Route 66, keeping watch for cars driving east that might be Gil and Wes returning from the hospital. She thought of her fascinating interview with Sterling who had painted a picture of what the hotel was like in the seventies. She thought about how everyone seemed so genuine when they told her they knew nothing of the shooting this morning. But that was just her stupid belief in people. *No, it isn't stupid to believe in the good in people,* she admonished herself.

Her thoughts then once again bounced back to Sterling's stories. He had told her a lot about the old hotel, but in particular, while she directed her questions to the late seventies, he mentioned a few items of interest that might help in her Dirk inquiry. He said that Tom was "madly and stupidly" in love with Julie. He mentioned that Gil was the hotel gossip. He also mentioned that Mr. and Mrs. Flint missed Annabelle terribly after she left to go to boarding school in California. Eve thought it was cute that, decades later, Walter's ex-employees still called him Mr. Flint. Sterling had talked a lot about Mr. Flint, how he was stern but always helpful, always there for anybody in need. Eve wished she could meet that version of Walter.

She caught sight of a lonely car in the distance. It looked like it could be her SUV and it looked like it was slowing down. She felt a wave of anticipation when the car did indeed pull onto the hotel's driveway. She knew she was being silly, but she had an overwhelming desire to lay eyes on Wes, to remind herself that he was truly fine. The entire day, she had been thinking about Wes being shot, and then Dirk, a man who looked so much like Wes, being shot dead. The two stories, the two images were getting tangled in her brain.

She walked to the parking lot to meet them, but when the car pulled up she saw only Gil. She tried her best to keep a look of placid contemplation on her face but inside she was in full-blown panic mode. Had Gil not immediately eased her mind she might have screamed.

"He's fine," Gil said as soon as he got out of the car. "I dropped him off at his girlfriend's ranch. He called her and told her what happened, and she insisted that she nurse him back to health. But he really is fine. He didn't even need stitches. I figured you wouldn't mind if he took the rest of the day off."

"Of course, no problem," Eve said as she focused on resuming her normal heartrate. She distractedly noticed a wet spot on Gil's pant leg.

"Well, well, well," he said as he looked down at the offensive spot. "I helped myself to some of that iced tea while I was driving. I guess I spilled some. But I don't think I got any on the seat or anything. Oh, I'll grab it and bring it back to the kitchen." He took the basket from the back seat, handed her the car keys, and quickly walked away.

Eve was still reeling from her shock at not seeing Wes.

She decided to call him. When he answered, a huge nonsensical weight was lifted from her worried soul. When Wes joked that June was treating him like a baby, Eve laughed far too loud. She was so happy, so relieved. He could take off as many days as he wanted, she told him.

Eve let her relief wash over her. She felt like a changed woman, like she could focus again. Perhaps she had been a tiny bit hysterical this morning and making wild connections.

Eve turned her thoughts to more practical matters as she walked back to the front of the hotel. When she entered the lobby, she found Julie waiting outside the office door.

"Hi," said Julie. "Are we still doing my history interview?"

"Yes. I'm sorry, I have a million things on my mind. But yes, I would like to do that. But first, I wanted to ask if Tom can help me take care of the horses since Wes is going to be out for a couple of days."

"He's already taken on the job," Julie said with a smile. "He's out there with them right now. It's pretty sweet, actually. I can tell he really misses being around horses. He becomes a much calmer, more grounded person around them."

"You just retired, right? Maybe you two should move out to the country."

Julie tilted her head in contemplation. "Hmmm. That's something to think about... Yes, I must admit that I might like that idea." She then jerked her gaze towards Eve and asked, "How is Wes? I just feel so bad. Is there anything I can do?"

"He's fine, thank you. Gil dropped him off at his girlfriend's place. It really was just a graze, thankfully."

"What a relief," Julie said with feeling.

Eve started her history interview with Julie but decided to ask her a series of the standard prepared questions before broaching the subject of Dirk. Just because Eve had decided to set aside the mystery of Wes's shooting, it didn't mean she wasn't still fascinated by the mystery of the murdered cowboy. When she felt that Julie was comfortable with the rhythm of the interview, Eve tried to gently switch to the subject of the murder.

"Tom and you met here?"

"Yes."

"You started dating here?"

"No. Tom had a huge crush on me. I thought he was a nice guy, but I was young and stupid and not interested in nice guys. He followed me around like a puppy dog. He thought I didn't notice.

"After the interstate was built," Julie continued, "no one drove Route 66 anymore, so there was no business at the hotel and it had to close. With no hotel, they didn't need a crew of maids, so I lost my job and moved to Las Vegas. Tom didn't lose his job because they still needed someone to care for the horses for Mr. Thorton and the horses the cowboys used on the ranch." Julie got a faraway look in her eyes and the corner of her mouth twitched upward. "But Tom said he couldn't stop thinking about me, so he quit his job and moved to Las Vegas. He moved just in case I might date him. How could I say no to that? We got married almost immediately, at one of those little wedding chapels on the Las Vegas Strip."

Eve hated to interrupt Julie's pleasant memories, but she had a plan. "So, if you weren't dating Tom while you lived here, were you dating anyone else?"

"No," Julie said, suddenly serious and guarded.

"Not Dirk?"

"No. I didn't even know him."

"Oh, I thought someone said that you liked him," Eve suggested.

"No, I didn't like him. I didn't know him. There were a lot of cowboys here. I worked in the hotel. The cowboys didn't come to the hotel."

Eve wanted to point out that the cowboys' bunkhouse was not too far from the cabins that Julie must have lived in, but she decided to drop that subject for now.

"Did you know Sterling? He was the gardener, so he would have been around the hotel."

"I mostly just spent time with the other maids, but yes, I remember Sterling. He was always very quiet. We girls thought he was a little strange. But it was unfair. Like I said, at that age, I did not make the wisest decisions when it came to boys. Sterling was probably the kind of guy that we should have been interested in, but at the time we thought he was a nerd because he always had his nose in a book or was inspecting the spots on a butterfly. And he was always taking pictures. I'm embarrassed to say, we made fun of him a lot behind his back. I hope he never knew. I was only 18 when I started working here. I was the youngest of all the girls working at the hotel, so a lot of the time, I just went along with what they thought so that I would fit in."

"Did you live out at the cabins? Did you share with the other girls?"

"Yes, we had a crew of four maids, and we all shared a cabin. It was tight, but we had fun."

"Who were in the other cabins?"

"The Flints in one; Millicent and Buck in one, us maids in one; Tom and the other horse wrangler, Eddie, shared a cabin. Sterling, I guess, I can't remember who he shared with. I think Gil drove in from Sandmat. But Millicent had two other kitchen helpers, Daisy and… I don't remember her name right now. Anyway, those girls shared a cabin."

"And the cowboys stayed in the bunkhouse?"

"Yes. I'm not sure how many bunks or cowboys there were. There was always a lot of turn over. Young men coming out to the ranch, wanting to try their hand at cowboying and then realizing it wasn't all eating beans out of a can by a campfire. When they realized it was back-breaking work they moved on to something else and somewhere else."

"Were any of the girls back then named Leslie by chance?"

"No, not Leslie. I remember Betty and Susan. I can't remember the other maid's name or the kitchen girl. I'm sure I would remember if I heard their names, but definitely not Leslie."

"And what about Gil? He worked in the kitchen in the hotel. Did you know him well?"

"Not really. He didn't live here, and we weren't allowed in the kitchen. Plus, again, we girls thought he was weird because he worked in the kitchen. At the time, we thought being a cook was a job for women. Which is so funny to think about now. Nowadays, in the restaurants I worked at in Las Vegas at least, if you don't have an overbearing egotistical man running the kitchen who is constantly screaming orders at people, it's not considered a good restaurant! Times have changed."

Eve was no longer concerned about her investigation. She was having fun hearing the opinions of the Arizona Sunset Ranch Hotel maids. "And what about Ramon? Do you remember him at all?"

"Yes, now that I've had some time to think, I do remember him a little, but he wasn't here long, but that reminds me… the position he held, the busboy/bellhop job… I think that is who Sterling bunked with. Not Ramon, because I think he drove in from Sandmat, maybe with Gil sometimes. But the other young men who had that job, that's who Sterling shared a cabin with. That's right… when Ramon worked here, Sterling had the cabin to himself, and we girls thought they should put him in with Tom and Eddie and give the cabin to two of us so we could have more space. Big time ranch politics!" Julie started laughing.

Eve laughed with her. It was nice to take a quick mental break from the stress of the day.

Chapter Nineteen

After Julie left, Eve decided to take her usual walk down the driveway. She hadn't been able to do it this morning since she had woken up late. She relied on those morning walks to sort her thoughts and appreciate life. She realized that her simple walk every morning with Sunset helped to keep her sane. '*I believe this is the place that restores my sanity.*' That is what her Great Aunt Genevieve had said in her diary. Eve agreed with her aunt. There was something truly magical about the wide-open spaces of this valley.

So, to catch up on her much-needed dose of sanity today, Eve walked. She walked all the way down the driveway to Historic Route 66 and back to the hotel, a total of almost two miles. On her walk, she ruminated on her flustered state of mind after having slept in this morning. Perhaps if she had been more composed this morning, she would have handled the bizarre and shocking event differently — better. Or perhaps, the entire sequence of events would have changed, and Wes would not have been shot... *Stop that!* Eve reprimanded her inner dialogue.

There was no point in thinking of what-ifs. It was childish, pointless, and self-abusive. *When an unfortunate event happens, you need to own the reality of the situation and come up with solutions, not dwell on the alternate timelines of fantasy.* It was not the first time she had had this conversation with herself, and she supposed it would not be the last.

On her return, she saw that Ramon and Gil had stationed themselves on two of the four rocking chairs on the front porch. She took a moment to enjoy the beautiful moment, seeing the men enjoying an iced tea together in the location where they met almost half a century ago. This reunion that she had organized created this moment. Good moments were happening all around her. She desperately wanted to focus only on the good but as she neared the hotel, she knew she must deal with the bad. Eve needed to have a serious and private discussion with Gil.

Ramon being there was the next best thing to catching Gil alone. In fact, perhaps it was better. Eve trusted Ramon implicitly and his take on Gil's answers to Eve's questions might be helpful since the two men were close friends. He may have an insight that Eve lacked. She quickened her step to make sure she caught them before today's barbecue started.

Although she decided not to beat around the bush, she spoke calmly and quietly.

"Gil, now that we have a moment to talk and we both have had plenty of time to think about the events of this morning, I would like to ask you a question."

Gil looked uncomfortable but said, "Okay."

"Do you think the person who murdered Dirk tried to murder you?" she asked.

"No. No way," he said confidently as he shook his head.

"No?"

"No. It couldn't be. That's impossible," Gil said

110

resolutely.

"Impossible? Who do you think killed Dirk?"

"Well... I... I don't feel comfortable saying. I shouldn't have made that comment to Ben last night. I'm embarrassed that I did and that you all heard it. I don't want to make it worse by saying anything more."

"But you don't think that the person who shot at you could possibly be the same person who killed Dirk?"

"No, I really don't think so."

"You said it was impossible."

"Well, I'm not one hundred percent sure, but I don't think so, no." Gil stood up. "I'm sorry. I'm not trying to be difficult. I just think that it would be best if we let things lie and moved on. I'm going to go get some more iced tea." He opened the large front door and went inside.

Eve did not expect him to return. She sat down in his vacant seat.

"That conversation yielded absolutely nothing," said Ramon.

"It was vague and strange and, yes, not particularly helpful," Eve mused, "but I wouldn't say 'nothing.' We learned that Gil was just guessing at Dirk's murderer, and he may have been wrong."

Ramon shot Eve a look that she couldn't interpret.

"What?" she asked.

"Everyone seems to think that Wes's shooting was an accident," said Ramon. "Not that you should believe something based on public opinion, but... Perhaps it was."

"I know, I know," Eve said with a sigh. "Maybe I just let my imagination run wild by trying to connect the two shootings. Everyone else seems to think that's a crazy idea."

"I never said it was crazy," Ramon said kindly.

"Thank you, but maybe it is. I should probably take everyone's advice to be content that no one was seriously injured and let the matter lie."

"Can you do that?"

"Maybe. I mean, the most obvious explanation was that it was probably Ben, like Millicent suggested. That would account for Julie and Tom's strange behavior. They probably know the shooting had something to do with their irresponsible son. And even though he is lying to protect himself, he probably learned his lesson. Hopefully."

The two shared a moment of contemplative silence.

"I need to go see if Esperanza needs anything," Ramon said apologetically.

"Of course!" said Eve.

"I have been dealing with a confusing and overwhelming guilt playing the part of a guest while my sainted wife is working," he further explained.

"You're fine. Go."

"Plus, I must admit, I am ravenous, and I want to ensure the timely commencement of this barbecue!" Ramon winked at her as he stood up.

"Thank you," she said.

As Ramon headed inside the hotel, Eve stayed seated to relax– for just a minute, she told herself. A moment later, the front door opened, and Daisy walked out.

"Oh, hi," Daisy said. "I was going to my home to get a few things for my room." She walked across the porch and down the steps before she turned around and asked, "Would you like to see it?"

"Your home?"

"Yes."

"I'd love to," Eve said as she rose from her chair. She had always been fascinated by the idea of living in a truly mobile home. Her mother had moved Eve and her brother, Logan, around a lot when they were children. Young Eve had become accustomed to packing and unpacking their few belongings each time they relocated, but she always wondered what it might be like to bring your whole house with you when you moved.

She followed Daisy to the parking lot to an older RV with rudimentary daisies painted on the side of it.

"I love your daisy caravan, Daisy," Eve said with a smile. Admittedly, a bit of an anglophile, Eve preferred the English term 'caravan' over 'RV' and allowed this one little English-ism in her speech. After all, she was constantly stopping herself from using the words lift and torch to replace the American versions, elevator and flashlight, to prevent people from considering her strange or pretentious. But she had decided some years ago that caravan was just a far superior word than RV (which wasn't even really a word), therefore she chose to formally adopt it.

As they entered the rolling world of Daisy, Eve couldn't help but think that it must be a visual representation of the resident's mind: colorful, comforting, and scattered.

As Eve watched Daisy search for her belongings, Eve decided that since Daisy herself was a little off beat, perhaps she wouldn't mind being asked an unexpected question.

"Daisy?"

"Yes?"

"Who do you think shot Wes this morning?" Eve asked her casually.

"I thought it was obvious," an unbothered Daisy replied as she continued to open cabinets and retrieve her things. "It's the same person who killed Dirk."

Finally! Someone agrees with me! "And who do you think that is?" Eve waited with bated breath.

"Ernest."

Eve let out a very disappointed sigh. "Ernest, the ghost?"

"Yes," Daisy said confidently. "It's the only person that makes sense when you think about it."

Chapter Twenty

The poolside barbeque was fun. Everyone— save Walter, who was in his room taking a nap— enjoyed playing a heated game of horseshoes. Walter's attentive daughter would periodically sneak off to go check on him. A little more than periodically, Eve thought. Annabelle seemed to be in good spirits and enjoying herself until each time she reminded herself to go check on her father. Eve thought the poor lady was running herself ragged and could use some time to relax. Eventually, Eve suggested that she go check on Walter instead, but Gil jumped up and offered. And the next time, Sterling offered. Annabelle seemed happy with this set up and helped herself to a mojito.

When Sterling returned, he had Walter with him.

"He woke up," Sterling said simply to Annabelle.

Walter looked like he was still half asleep. He turned to Sterling and said, "Do you have the rifle?"

"What rifle?" Sterling scratched at his facial scar. "Are you thinking about when I was the shooting range guide? Remember that, Mr. Flint? I was always carrying rifles around back then. But not anymore. My gun days are over. The only shooting I do these days is with my camera."

As Sterling spoke, Walter listened and began to nod instinctively. By the time Sterling was finished, Walter looked awake and seemed to be nodding intently. "No more guns," he said.

"Are you hungry, Dad?" asked Annabelle.

Walter nodded again.

"I thought so. Let's get you some food. It's so good, I wish I could eat more, but I'm stuffed."

Loretta offered to get a plate together for Walter, but Annabelle said she would do it since she knew what he liked.

Eve wanted to take advantage of the mention of the shooting range. She turned to the rest of the group and said, "So, Sterling told me that the hotel guests really loved the target shooting. It's too bad it had to get shut down."

"You could always open it back up," Ben said logically.

Oops, that wasn't the right thing to say! Oh well, I guess I have to go with it… Eve thought before she said, "Maybe I should. After all, if your guests really liked it, maybe mine would too."

"Yeah, the guests loved it," said Tom. "It made them feel like they were in the Wild West. For a lot of them, it's the only time they ever shot a gun in their life. That's why we needed Sterling to show them how to shoot. They did not know what they were doing."

"Did you use the range, Tom?" asked Eve.

"Everybody did," said Julie. "It's not like there was a lot to do out here."

"Were you a good shot, Dad?" asked Ben.

"No, I never got very good," replied Tom.

"Who was the best out of all of you?" asked Ben.

"Well, Sterling, probably," said Gil.

"Maybe," said Sterling, "but Annabelle was pretty

good."

"Oh, that's right," interjected Eve. "Walter said something about her being a good shot, and Ramon told me that she won competitions." She purposefully neglected telling them that she saw a picture of Annabelle winning a trophy in the newspaper archive when Eve was researching them all.

Annabelle walked back to the group and set the plate of food in front of Walter. "Are you all talking about my childhood shooting skills? That's so funny to think about now. I was obsessed with target shooting when I was a kid. Winning the Sheriff's Sharpshooting Trophy was the highlight of my life. And you always helped with that competition, didn't you, Sterling?"

"Yes. In fact, that's how I got the job here." Sterling turned to Eve. "I failed to mention this in my history interview because it is the story I was saving for tonight, for the filming."

"Well, please tell it now," Eve prodded. "We'll call it a rehearsal."

"Okay. The Sheriff's Sharpshooting Competition was an old tradition in the area," began Sterling. "The Sheriff's Department would hold a shooting competition for children from 10 to 17 years old. The tradition had been established long before as a recruitment technique for the department to see what children in the area might be suited for a life in law enforcement. I won the competition when I was 16 and again when I was 17. After that, I helped organize the event. Even though it was an antiquated idea that the winner would become local law enforcement, Sheriff Weed really liked me and wanted me to join the Sheriff's Department. In fact, I think he wanted to groom me to be his replacement. I always wondered if I should have done it. But at the time I had no interest. When Sheriff Weed finally accepted that, he suggested to Mr. Flint that I be a shooting range guide out here at the ranch. Then, when Annabelle started winning all the shooting competitions, everyone assumed it was due to my exceptional tutelage. But it wasn't. Annabelle just had natural talent and an obsession with shooting."

Annabelle laughed. "I did! I practiced all the time. But after I went off to boarding school, that all stopped. I guess I never really thought about the fact that the shooting range had closed down, because when I came back for holidays and summers, I just wasn't interested in that anymore. Did you get laid off when it closed down, Sterling? I don't remember."

"No, I was still here until the hotel closed. Which was, I think about a year, maybe a year and a half later. I still had plenty to do taking care of the grounds, the pool, the vegetable garden, and the orchard."

"Orchard?" Eve asked.

"There used to be fruit trees over there." Gil pointed to the southeast corner of the property. "What happened to them?"

"We had to cut them down after they got some disease," said Millicent.

"That's what you get for laying me off," joked Sterling.

Everyone chuckled. As Eve looked around at the smiling faces pleasantly reminiscing, she wondered how she could have ever thought that any of them would have tried to intentionally shoot Gil this morning. It seemed like such an absurd idea now.

"It was pretty neat back then," said Gil. "We had meat, milk, vegetables, and fruit all on the property. We were farm to table before it was trendy."

"Don't forget my eggs," said Millicent.

"That's right," said Annabelle. "Millie loved her chickens."

Everyone had something to say about those chickens. As the group talked and laughed about Millicent's chicken coop, Eve watched Walter eat. He seemed to be particularly enjoying the potato salad, so Eve went and got him some more. She sat down next to him to keep him company while he ate.

Eve couldn't help but wonder if Walter knew who killed Dirk. She kept thinking of his strange question from yesterday, "Where's the killer?" He had been staring out at the empty horse pasture when he said it. Who was he looking for? Tom would be the most likely person to be in the horse pasture since he was the horse wrangler back then. The more she thought about it, the more she was certain that Walter probably knew, or at least had an idea, who shot and killed Dirk. Walter had been in charge of the property. It was his job to take care of problems. And Millicent said he knew everything that went on around here. But Eve certainly couldn't interrogate the poor man.

Chapter Twenty-One

Since the big meal for the day was the afternoon barbecue, the only thing left on the agenda was "Storytime" this evening. Eve was looking forward to her event in which she planned to film each of the old hotel employees telling their favorite story from their time working at the Arizona Sunset Ranch Hotel. She had hopes to cut some of the filmed stories, audio history interviews, and pictures of the property to make a short documentary film about the history of the hotel and ranch. She thought it might be fun to show the film in the evenings in the lobby as informative entertainment.

Before Storytime, everyone had some free time to relax and get ready for their big film debut. Eve went to her office and prepared her new documentary film camera. She now only needed to go set up the area in the lobby where the filming would take place. But she had a little time and decided to use it to scan some more photos.

She came upon her new favorite picture. It was a uniquely wonderful photograph of both the hotel staff and ranch staff standing in front of the hotel waving to Annabelle as she was about to get into a car. It was one of

Millicent's photos. The back of the picture read, *Annabelle off to boarding school September 1, 1977*. And not only did it feature the entirety of the people that lived and worked on the property, but it also included Mr. Thorton and Aunt Genevieve. This was truly a special picture that featured everyone, except for Millicent, who took the photo. Eve would need to thank Millicent for having the foresight to take this wonderful group photo.

She studied all the tiny faces, picking out the young versions of each of her current guests. She wanted to get a better look, so she walked over to the window to open the blinds. She stopped when she heard the creak of the rocking chair on the other side of the window. She didn't want to open the blinds and take away the privacy of whomever had just sat down on the porch. When voices drifted in, she realized that the window was cracked open. She could hear every word of what was obviously supposed to be a private conversation. Eve quickly deduced that it was Millicent and Annabelle.

"Where's your dad?" asked Millicent.

"Sterling and Tom took him out to see the horses."

"That's nice. He'll like that. And it's nice for you to have a break."

"Yes, but I always worry when he's out of my sight. Especially now since… since the incident about a month ago."

"Uh oh, that doesn't sound good."

"It could have been worse, I guess. We were at the grocery store and I lost him. When I finally found him he was standing over a man that he had just pushed down. I still don't know what happened exactly. Maybe the man was rude to Dad or maybe Dad confused him for someone else, I really don't know. But Dad pushed him, and the man fell backwards and bruised his tail bone. He was in a fit to press charges. He called the police immediately. It was horrible."

"How old was this man?"

"Well, that's the thing," Annabelle chuckled sadly. "When the man realized that Dad was a good 30 years older than him, I think he got embarrassed about being physically overpowered by an elderly man and withdrew his claims of being a poor defenseless victim."

"Walter is very physically fit for his age," commented Millicent.

"I know, it's so sad that his mind isn't. I'm afraid his condition has seemed to worsen after arriving here. Or maybe it just seems like it because we're somewhere different. No, it's worse. I know it is. It's sad. I think this is the last trip we'll ever be able to take. I just wish it would have been better. I was hoping that being here would be good for him, good for his memory. I thought he would remember the happy times here with mom. But being here might be confusing him even more. I don't know. It's hard."

Eve felt so sorry for Annabelle. She could tell the stress of being a full-time caretaker was getting to her. Even since her arrival, Annabelle's naturally joyous personality seemed to dampen considerably. Eve had noticed at the barbecue that Annabelle was nervously chewing on her nicely manicured fingernails.

"I'm sorry you have to deal with that, honey. I thought coming back here would be good for me too. I thought it would make me miss Buck less. Maybe I would get some of that... what do you call it?"

"Closure?"

"Yes, closure. But being here is just making me miss him more. It's making me miss the good old days."

"It was fun here, wasn't it?"

"Yes, we had some good times," Millicent said sadly. "Lots of good times. That's why I wish we could have just remembered those. I wish that scoundrel, Dirk, wouldn't have come up."

A few moments of silence passed before Annabelle said, "So, what exactly happened? I never knew anything about it."

"Just between us... Dirk stole a couple of head of cattle. There was no proof that Dirk did it, but we all knew he did it. I had never seen Buck so angry. I was blind with rage myself. To steal from the hand that feeds you... it was just atrocious. Buck was going to fire him and... and the next thing I knew Dirk was dead. Buck was always real quiet on the subject. He never mentioned Dirk ever again. I was always afraid he..." Millicent trailed off with emotion.

"It's okay, Millie. It's all in the past."

Annabelle changed the subject and asked Millicent what she had been up to for the last 25 years since she had seen her. The two went back and forth catching up on a lot of lost time.

Eve could still hear them just as well, but she had stopped listening. She was trying to discern what exactly Millicent had meant. The way she worded her account of Dirk's death could be taken a few different ways.

Suddenly, Eve remembered her schedule to film. She needed to get that set up. She got her things together as quietly as possible so Millicent and Annabelle wouldn't hear her through the open window and realize their privacy had been compromised. Eve couldn't help but laugh at herself. Maybe she had deserved all those elementary school eavesdropping jokes.

.

Chapter Twenty-Two

Everyone had convened for Storytime, save Loretta and Roxie who Eve sent home to rest up and Ben who was in his room. He said he would "wait for the movie."

As Storytime commenced, Eve asked Sterling to be the first to tell his story since he had already warmed up earlier. He told the story about how he secured a position here as the shooting range guide and then proceeded to tell another story about how Mr. Flint found more and more work for him to do. At first Sterling thought he was being punished by the increasing workload. But Sterling eventually realized that his mounting responsibilities were because Mr. Flint trusted him. When he realized that he had not only earned Mr. Flint's trust but also his respect, this gave Sterling a confidence that he had never experienced before. A confidence that stayed with him his entire life, and the importance of which he never forgot. When he finished, Sterling thanked Walter for being the most meaningful father figure in his life. Walter stood up, walked over to Sterling and shook his hand. Eve was embarrassed that she had started crying until she looked around the room and realized she wasn't the only one.

There wasn't a dry eye in the house.

She was so happy that she not only experienced this touching moment, but she just recorded it! Her original plan had been to stop and start the filming, but she realized she might as well leave the camera running. Maybe she would get something impromptu that she would want to use.

She imagined that no one would want to follow such a moving story, but she was wrong. She was surprised to find that, not only did everyone have a touching story, but all the stories were about Walter or both Walter and his wife, Constance.

Julie told a story about the maids getting into some mischief and getting in big trouble with Mrs. Flint. But Mr. Flint talked his wife down, saying they were just girls and should be able to have a little fun.

Millicent told a story about one Christmas Eve in the 1980s when it was just Walter, Constance, Millicent and Buck on the property. They had been snowed in for days and Millicent had a breakdown because all she wanted for Christmas was to make a pie, but she had no sugar. Buck told her she was being ridiculous, and she knew she was, but Walter mounted his favorite horse and rode for miles to the next ranch and came back with sugar for her.

Tom told a story about how the first and last time he was ever bucked off a horse was on his second day at work here. He was so embarrassed and was sure he was going to get fired for his inexperience. Mrs. Flint was the only one who witnessed his embarrassing moment and she told him that she would keep his secret. But Tom always suspected she must have told her husband. Mr. Flint would come out at least once a day and give just one casual, discreet suggestion on how to handle the horses properly. Tom said the Flints were so good at teaching the young adults how to do their jobs in a way that made them feel good about themselves.

Gil told the story about how he had come to the ranch

for a job as a cowboy, but the ranch wasn't hiring. Gil really needed a job, so Buck sent him over to Walter at the hotel. The only position they needed to fill was cook's assistant. Gil explained that Mr. Flint was reticent to hire him, but Gil pleaded. Walter finally took pity on the pathetic, young, broke man and he gave him the job. And by doing so, Mr. Flint changed the course of Gil's life. Gil found that he loved cooking. Millicent was a great teacher and after he was laid off from the hotel, he knew he wanted to start his own restaurant. He has now been the proud owner of Dancer Diner, a Sandmat institution for 38 years. And it was all because Walter took a chance on him.

Ramon told a story about sliding down the rail of one of the staircases when he thought he was alone. When he realized that Mr. and Mrs. Flint were both at the bottom of the stairs, Ramon held his breath for his punishment. After a moment of silence, Mrs. Flint started laughing uncontrollably. Mr. Flint kept a straight face as he sternly said, "That is the last time you are going to do that, correct?" Ramon said he nodded his head so violently he thought it might fall off. But right before Mr. Flint took his wife's arm to walk her away, Ramon saw him crack a smile.

The stories painted a picture of a very serious man who was secretly kind, and his very kind wife who was secretly serious. They sounded like a wonderful couple. Annabelle had cried so much hearing such lovely stories about her parents, Eve told her she did not have to feature her tear-stained face and puffy eyes on film this evening. Perhaps they could do one later, with her and her dad at their convenience later this weekend.

Eve was about to call the official end of Storytime when Walter started talking. It appeared that all the stories had jogged his memory and he wanted to share a story as well. As he began speaking Eve discreetly moved the camera to the direction where Walter was sitting.

"You know, we started making wine here after the hotel closed," he said.

Eve was so excited to hear a story from Walter's perspective. She prompted him to continue by saying, "How did that come about?"

"In the late 1970s, it occurred to people that if they could successfully make good wine in California, they should also be able to do it in Arizona," Walter began. "Mr. Thorton had a friend down in Willcox who was part of a group that wanted to make Arizona into a wine production state. One night while that friend was staying at the ranch here, they got into a debate whether Northern Arizona or Southern Arizona would produce the best wine. They made a bet and in 1979, Mr. Thorton planted the vineyard and became one of the pioneer Arizona vineyard owners."

Eve was impressed with Walter's narrative. She thought it likely that he had given this speech hundreds of times over the years and that it must be ingrained in his consciousness.

"Up until then," Walter continued, "there were some antiquated Arizona laws that prohibited wineries from selling directly to other businesses or to the public. But Mr. Thorton worked with the other winemakers and in 1981 they helped pass a law which allowed Arizona wineries to open tasting rooms and sell directly to customers. So, we set up a nice tasting room in the dining room here. We didn't get too many people making it all the way out here, mostly other wine aficionados, but it was enough that we opened the hotel rooms up to those who wanted to do wine tastings and spend the night."

Eve was thrilled to learn this information. "What was the wine called? What did the bottles look like? I've been trying to locate information, but I haven't been successful."

"Arizona Sunset Ranch Wines," Walter said.

"What varietals did you grow?" asked Julie.

"We grew a lot of different grapes. The reds were Syrah, Zinfandel, Carménère, Cabernet Sauvignon. And the whites were Roussanne, Chardonnay, and Vignoles."

"Who won the bet?" asked Tom.

"That was a bet Mr. Thorton lost, but it took him a good five to six years to finally concede. Wine production proved to be less problematic in Willcox."

After that, Walter rubbed his tired eyes. After having spent the last couple of days with him, everyone knew the signs that he had lost his connection to that memory. The questions stopped. Eve was so tired herself she was amazed that Walter had not only stayed up this late, but had such a wonderful and informative moment of clarity.

"Is it my turn?" asked Daisy.

Eve felt horrible. She had forgotten to include Daisy in the line up since she was a late arrival. Daisy was already such an outsider, Eve didn't want to make her feel self-conscious.

"Yes, I saved the best for last!" Eve said. Luckily, Daisy was sitting next to Walter, so she was already in the camera shot. "Just look into the camera and tell an interesting story about when you worked here."

"Ok," she said. Daisy then turned and looked deeply into the eye of the camera. "It is the story of my missing lipstick. I bought the most beautiful lipstick at the drugstore. I loved it so much. But then it went missing. It was the first time I knew Ernest was real. I — "

"Don't be daft, Daisy!" Millicent nearly shouted. "Ernest isn't real. Buck and I made him up to keep the cowboys in line. I mean it seemed pretty obvious, didn't it? We named him Ernest to keep y'all earnest."

"What? That's horrible!" Daisy exclaimed.

"Why? It worked. Mostly." Millicent countered.

"But I saw his grave," said Daisy.

"Two sticks some of the older cowboys nailed together and hammered into the ground to mess with the newcomers," Millicent explained.

"But my lipstick was gone. I know it was Ernest. He was punishing me for sneaking extra food to Dirk," Daisy said softly as she looked down in shame.

"You were the one who was giving him food out of my kitchen?" Millicent asked angrily. "I should have done more than take your lousy lipstick!"

"You took my lipstick?"

"I was doing you a favor. It was too red, and you didn't know the first thing about applying makeup. You looked like a pathetically inexperienced street walker." Millicent stood up and shook her head in frustration. She marched up to her room without saying goodnight.

It had been such a long day. Eve let everyone know that there were snacks and drinks in the dining room if anyone needed anything, but she was exhausted and needed to go to bed. Esperanza and Ramon offered to double check everything before they went home to their cabin.

Before leaving, Eve went over to Daisy and kindly suggested that they film a story of hers at some other time this weekend when everyone wasn't so tired.

Daisy nodded her head in acceptance. She then leaned in and whispered in Eve's ear, "But just so you know, Ernest is real. He really does punish the wicked. The people here need to be careful."

Chapter Twenty-Three

Eve went to her room and got ready for bed with thoughts of Ernest filling her head. She was in her pajamas and pulling back her comforter by the time she remembered she had forgotten the camera. She had not just forgotten to remove it from the lobby, she had forgotten to turn it off. Where was her mind?

She put on a robe and snuck back into the lobby, hoping she wouldn't run into anyone. She was in luck. The dimly lit lobby was vacant. Everyone must have been tired as well. Even though she had woken up late this morning, Eve felt like today had been one of the longest days of her life.

She turned off the camera and brought it and the tripod into her suite. As Eve settled in for the night, she tried to focus on the good things that happened today, but it was hard not to fixate on Wes getting shot.

She turned to Genevieve's diaries for distraction. She picked up the 1977 diary. She looked for late August, early September entries. She read the one dated August 30th:

I cannot believe that as a young woman I considered becoming a nurse. What a tragic mistake that would have been!

I am loath to be around the ill for fear of falling ill myself. How could I have possibly have ever cared for them?

Today, I came upon poor Daisy retching at the side of the building. I was immediately concerned that I might incur influenza and have my entire recreation time ruined by illness. I insisted, kindly I hope, that she immediately return to her cabin. Luckily, Leslie was close at hand and took her home.

The experience concerned me. Have I become a dreadful person? Perhaps I should endeavor to restore the altruism of my youth.

Eve felt connected to her great aunt in a new way. In college, Eve had studied human behavior with the thought that she would be a therapist of some sort, helping people with their psychological and emotional health. But she too had grown out of her selfless phase and chose a life without the strain of being constantly encumbered with the depression and problems of others. And she too felt guilty about that from time to time.

She then read the next day, August 31st:

Annabelle's goodbye party was today. Early tomorrow she will be off on her new adventure. What a whirlwind for the young thing. I truly hope she will be happy at her new school in California. Perhaps it will be best for her to be around others her own age. I assured her that she will make loads of friends and will have a joyous time. I believe her departure tomorrow morning will be more upsetting for the staff here at the hotel and ranch. I know she will be missed by all.

Children are a blessing in more ways than one. It is enjoyable to have the limitless happiness and energy of youth present in one's life. It is a reminder to us all to enjoy the simple things in life and not get bogged down by the numerous drudgeries of adulthood. Yes, young Annabelle's infectious smile and joie de vivre will be missed.

Eve thought how fortuitous it was to be reading this entry the same day that she had just come upon the picture of everyone waving goodbye to young Annabelle the day after the party. She actually had a picture to go with this diary entry. *How cool is that?* Daisy must not have had the flu because Eve remembered that she was included in the group waving goodbye to Annabelle.

Eve felt her eyelids becoming heavy and welcomed the idea of sleep. She closed the diary and set it down on her nightstand, but as she leaned to turn off the light, something struck her, and she was once again wide awake.

Annabelle's going away party was at the end of August. Annabelle had said Dirk's death must have been after she had left for school that year. But it wasn't. Annabelle was still here at the time Dirk had been shot, killed, and quickly forgotten.

But certainly, it didn't mean anything. Like Annabelle had said during her history interview: she had been a child, a mysterious death on the property is something that would have been kept from her.

Eve was mad at herself for letting the meaningless revelation prevent her from falling asleep. But she knew the moment of fatigue had passed and she might be looking at a long night of insomnia. She quickly picked up the diary again in hopes reading it would once again calm her into slumberland.

She read some random entries from the beginning of the diary. As she read a particularly interesting entry about a business trip to Rome, she mused on the concept of writing a diary. Why did Genevieve choose to journal her life? Was it a form of stress relief? A way to remember her life? Eve had never considered journaling, but she would certainly like to remember things from her life that she had forgotten. And as she grew older, she would forget even more. It might be nice to have a record of her life, just for herself. And who knows, perhaps one day, one of her nieces would read through them and find them fascinating. Yes, perhaps she should. She had a few blank journals she had received as gifts over the years. She had only ever used the pages for hurried to-do lists when she couldn't find any other scratch paper.

The more she thought of the idea, the more merit she gave it. She got up and found one of the blank journals and one of her favorite ball point pens. She got back into bed feeling like a silly teenager who was going to pour out an emotional drama about the boys she liked. She giggled as she wrote "Dear Diary," and then paused. She became serious as she wrote the date.

She began to chronicle her day. The more she wrote, the more she had to say. Writing down the events of the day was proving to be helpful. She was looking at the incidents from a different perspective, reanalyzing what she had seen, what she had heard.

After an hour of writing, Eve felt satisfied that she had captured the essence of the day, if not every detail. After all, it had been an incredibly long, event-filled day. And now that she had taken the thoughts out of her head and placed them on paper, she was tired enough to finally fall asleep.

Chapter Twenty-Four

Eve had started her day extra early. She had not slept well. One of the reasons was due to the building of a sinus headache. She had hoped the monsoons had come to an end but the pressure in her head was proof that they were due for another storm soon. But the main culprit preventing her peaceful sleep had been the nagging thoughts of shootings, past and present.

In the early hours of the morning, she had tried to soothe herself with happy thoughts, focusing on Walter's unexpected and informative Arizona Sunset Ranch Wines story. She had tried to remember the grape varietals and had thought of her future endeavor with Naiya. *Old vines seemed to be a coveted thing in the wine industry,* she had thought to herself. *Perhaps it was going to be successful.* Eve had tried to determine the age of the vines. *Although some of them were probably planted throughout the eighties and nineties, Walter said the first planting was in… 1979. So that would make them… Wait.* A recent memory had flashed in her mind.

She had remembered that right after the shooting she had asked Daisy where she had been when she heard the gunshot. When Daisy replied that she was in the vineyard because she had always loved walking through the rows of vines, Tom gave her a strange look. Now, Eve realized why. Daisy stopped working here in 1977 when there were no grape vines yet planted. That realization had led to a fitful sleep the rest of the night.

Eve was in the lobby having a cup of coffee, looking at the stacks of old photos of the hotel. The hotel was quiet, and she was enjoying having the place to herself for a few moments. Because it was so early, she assumed everyone was still asleep. Therefore, it unsettled her when she heard the front door open.

Sterling walked in with his ever-present duffel bag and set it on the floor. This time when he opened it, he took out a small box and handed it to Eve. "This one fell behind the seat in my car and I missed it."

Eve opened the box to find more photos of the hotel from the seventies. At the same moment, she was both delighted and overwhelmed. The thought of having more photos to scan exhausted her. Maybe she could get one of her employees to help her, but they were already so busy. Perhaps it had been a mistake to not hire at least one more person.

Sterling went into the dining room. Eve listened as he made himself a coffee and then heard the back door open and close. Off birding, Eve assumed.

His foray out into nature inspired her to do the same. She would go take her walk, even though she would miss Sunset. Perhaps her fence bird would keep her company. Ignoring the fact that she had told herself she would start jogging instead of walking, she walked her normal pace down the driveway to Historic Route 66. It was early, but it was already ramping up to be a hot and humid day. *Very humid – for here,* she thought. She had noticed that after moving to the high desert, her tolerance for humidity had decreased as substantially as her need for lotion had increased.

As she walked, she looked for her bird friend but didn't see him. Perhaps he was out posing for pictures for Sterling, the bird paparazzo. Her only companion this morning was Creeping Jenny, the vining weed that twirled up the fence. Ramon had told her that Field Bindweed (a.k.a. Creeping Jenny) was a non-native plant and considered a noxious weed in Arizona but Eve didn't care, she liked it. The thin stems were so industrious, twisting their way up and around the fences. The arrowhead leaves added extra green to her view and the delicate white trumpet-shaped flowers it produced were just lovely. In fact, Eve liked the plant even more after Ramon had told her it was non-native. After all, so was Eve. She and Jenny had that in common, non-native, but both thriving in this environment. Eve just hoped that no one considered her to be a noxious weed.

Weed… that reminded her of Ben laughing at Sheriff Weed's name. She wondered if perhaps the current sheriff could lend some insight into the past sheriff who had so quickly dismissed the suspicious death of a young cowboy. She thought about calling Sheriff Strider but decided it would be rude to call this early.

She went back inside and plopped back down in front of her pictures.

She opened her new box of treasures that Sterling had given her earlier. She casually sifted through the pictures until one in particular caught her eye. Someone's eye caught her eye, in fact. Young Tom's eye — Tom's black eye. The picture was a close-up shot of Tom grooming a horse, but he had a noticeably dark ring around his left eye. It reminded her of another picture. Eve sifted through the other pictures and found what she was looking for. It was the picture of Annabelle going off to boarding school when the entire staff was waving goodbye to her. Eve had noticed that Tom had a mark on his face. She thought it might have been a speck of dust on the negative when the picture was printed, or perhaps some dirt on his face but she realized it was the same shape as the black eye in this picture, but not as pronounced. It had been healing up on the day of Annabelle's departure for boarding school.

She heard a door close upstairs. She looked up. It was Annabelle. She came down the stairs wearing another striking outfit. Eve really liked Annabelle's style. Eve smiled at Annabelle as she walked into the dining room to get coffee. Eve hoped she would look that good in 20 years. Annabelle must have packed a lot of clothes for this trip. She never had on the same outfit twice and they were all perfect for every occasion, like her red and white horseback riding outfit. Except for that all black hiking outfit, that had not been perfect for the occasion, not at all.

Wait, thought Eve. *Yesterday, she told me that the horsehair on her pants must have been from the day before, but she wasn't wearing the same pants. She hadn't repeated any outfits. She had on red pants when she went horseback riding and black pants when she went hiking. How did she get horsehair on them? And why lie about it?*

Eve's phone rang. It was her mother. She usually spoke with her mother often, but she had been so busy lately it had been over a week since she had last checked in. She decided she had better answer it before her mother started to worry and had helicopters circling the property looking for her. She answered with an apology for having been so busy.

"It's okay, honey," said the voice of Eve's mother, Minna. "No apology necessary. I do have a life you know. It's not like I'm a shut-in that lives for the phone calls of my children. Which is a good thing, because if I did, I suppose I would be dead."

"Mother! Honestly! Do parents take classes on how to give passive aggressive guilt trips? I mean, seriously, it's quite a skill you've honed."

"Oh, please darling, don't be so melodramatic. I'm just having fun with you. Anyway, I've decided that I want to go on a hot air balloon. I think you should have a hot air balloon festival at your hotel. Wouldn't that be fun?"

"So, let me get this straight… In order for you to come visit me, I'm going to have to throw together a festival. A festival with hot air balloons."

"Yes. They have a huge one in Albuquerque, but I'd rather not go there. I'd rather come visit you."

"Why don't you just come visit next week for my grand opening."

"Are you going to have hot air balloons?"

"I decided it was going to be a BYOHAB party."

"Pardon?"

"Bring your own hot air balloon party. So, if you want to show up with a hot air balloon then we'll have One."

"I just might."

"Sounds great."

"Did I tell you I started a meditation class? The instructor is very handsome and probably around your age."

"Well, I guess I could see the benefits of dating a man that knows how to keep you quiet."

"Genevieve!"

"What? Don't get so melodramatic, Mother. I'm just having fun with you."

"Oh, and I joined a book club but honestly, it's more like a celebrity magazine club, that's all those ladies seem to talk about. But they're nice enough and the coffee shop where we meet…"

As Eve listened to the details of her mother's daily life, Eve meandered outside to the front porch. At some point her mother mentioned someone leaving dirty footprints on her new carpet and Eve had a hard time paying attention to the rest of the conversation. After distractedly ending the phone call with a promise to talk to her soon, Eve walked out to her car. She had decided she wanted to go out to the old shooting range and look for footprints. It was ridiculous, she knew, but she couldn't shake the thought that finding the culprit who shot Wes might be easily determined by looking for footprints. After all, it was monsoon season. The semi-wet ground might have perfectly preserved some footprints. And it hadn't rained yesterday, so they might still be there. She laughed to herself that she was forgetting to bring her wool cape and oversized magnifying glass. But, ridiculous or not, she was going.

She got in her car and made a mental note of the mileage, as was her custom (or obsessive behavior, however you wanted to analyze it), and pulled out of the parking lot. As she began to drive north on the property, she looked at the mileage again. *That can't be right,* thought Eve. The mileage that had been driven since the last time she looked was not nearly enough for a trip to the hospital and back. That would have been at the very least a 126-mile round trip and the odometer read a difference of 59 miles. Taking into account the distance from the shooting range, it was more like a roundtrip of 54 miles. That was the distance of a roundtrip to Sandmat, not the hospital, which was in the opposite direction. Gil obviously did not take Wes to the hospital, and he lied to her about it. He must have taken him to his house or the drugstore in Sandmat to get bandages. But why? And why was everyone lying to her about everything?

Her frustration made her even more determined to find some incriminating footprints. That's why she was so disappointed when she finally made her way out to the spot that she thought the shooter might have been standing, she found her crime scene compromised. She was sure there were footprints, yes, dozens of them. But they would all be Sterling's, who had set up a bird watching station there, and Butterscotch's, whom he rode out. Of all the places on the 10,000-acre property, this is where he chose to set up?

She walked towards him with no real purpose, but since he had seen her, she thought it would be suspicious to turn around and walk away. As she slowly rambled in Sterling's direction, she became distracted by the ravens cawing loudly by the decrepit old barn.

"It's not a murder," Sterling said when she arrived to his location.

She gave him a look to convey her confusion.

"It's not a murder, it's an unkindness."

"What?" She wondered if he was talking about the shooting yesterday. No one was murdered and shooting someone is certainly unkind.

"A group of ravens is called an unkindness, not a murder," he explained.

"Oh."

"Some people think since ravens are similar to crows, you use the same term, but you don't."

"An unkindness," she repeated distractedly.

Chapter Twenty-Five

Her conversation with Sterling had been pleasant enough. After talking about how Butterscotch was such a wonderful horse and how she held a special place in Eve's heart as her first, Sterling directed the talk to birds. Eve half listened as she surreptitiously checked the ground for any sign of someone else's footprints. But, as she suspected, her trip had been in vain.

On the drive back from the old shooting range, her phone rang. She saw it was Sheriff Strider. She answered the call as she pulled into the parking area at the cabins and parked so that she could focus.

"Hello," she said. "I was going to call you earlier."

"Is everything okay? Are you alright?" he said worriedly.

"Yes, yes, I'm fine. I was just going to ask you if you knew Sheriff Weed."

"Oh," he said with a sigh of relief. "Wait… how old do you think I am?" he added jokingly.

"No," she laughed. "Not did you know him personally. I meant do you know of him? Have you heard any old stories about him? Tales passed down through the campfire stories of sheriff generations."

"No, I've only been the sheriff here for five years. I've seen his name on a plaque here at the office featuring past sheriffs of Juniper County, but that's about it. I'm here right now, let me see… It looks like Sheriff Langham Weed was the sheriff of Juniper County from January 1953 to December 1977. So, that's all my information on the man."

"Okay, thanks. I was just wondering."

"I wish I could be more help," he said.

"Well, it's interesting that he was the sheriff for such a long time. He was sheriff in the area for the entire time the hotel had been open, up until Dirk's murder. He must have had some sort of relationship with the people who worked here and trusted them when they lied to him. And it tells me that he did indeed retire shortly after the incident like I was told. It's nice to know that I was told the truth about something."

"And… not that it means anything in reference to this case, but times were different back then. Sheriffs were not held as accountable as they are these days. I haven't heard any stories about Sheriff Weed, but I've heard quite a few about his successor. It is shocking what that man got away with around here."

"Like what?" Eve asked theatrically.

"Like drinking and driving while on duty – a lot. Enough to crash at least one official vehicle. And yet, he stayed sheriff."

"Oh, yikes."

"Yeah. If Sheriff Weed had swept anything under the rug or preemptively closed a case, his successor was not one to bother looking into it." He paused before he said, "Are you sure you're okay? Do you need anything?"

"I'm fine. My head is just spinning with too many convoluted thoughts. But you don't need to be dragged into my crazy mind."

"It's fine by me. I happen to like your particular brand

of crazy. Remember, in my job, I see a lot worse of the really bad kind of crazy on a daily basis. Which is why I am not a naturally trusting person, and why I called."

"Oh?"

"I know that earlier I was dismissive about the possibility of foul play," he admitted apologetically. "The more I thought about it, the more I wondered if I should have taken the situation more seriously."

"Do you now think that there is something nefarious going on?" she asked, unsure whether or not she wanted him to say yes or no.

"I still think it was probably an accident, but I wanted to let you know that I did do some quick background checks on your guests. I just wanted to make sure that I did my due diligence."

"And?"

"And, rest assured, none of your current guests have recently escaped from an asylum for the criminally insane," he joked.

"So helpful," she said sarcastically. "You may need to refine your detective skills a little." She then turned serious. "Are you not going to tell me what you found?"

"If you want."

"I want."

"Okay, but it's nothing really interesting."

"I'd still like to know."

"Just don't read too much into anything."

As Eve listened to the rustle of papers on the phone, she wondered whether or not Sheriff Strider was breaking any major rules by telling her this information. Just in case, she would be sure to keep the following information to herself.

"Okay, and thank you," she said kindly. "I appreciate it."

"Here we are," Strider said. "So, all I could find on Daisy Malone were dozens of address changes over the years and a few last name changes, looks like marriages and then back to her original. Millicent Buchanan appears to have led a very boring life, I couldn't find anything on her. It looks like Sterling was a career military man. Ben collects speeding tickets for fun and now has a suspended license. Walter has a recent, but dismissed, assault charge. I couldn't find anything of interest on Tom or Julie Hayward. Gil is a model citizen and Annabelle..." he trailed off.

"What about Annabelle?" Eve asked slowly.

To Eve's surprise Sheriff Strider laughed. "Well, it's not criminal, not unless you really hate politicians."

"Excuse me?"

"Did you know that Annabelle is a city council member in her affluent suburb of Phoenix? It's quite a high-profile position."

"No, I didn't know that. I just knew that she was taking a leave of absence from work for awhile to care for her father. Speaking of her father, do you have the details on that assault charge?"

"I couldn't find much on it, but since it was dismissed, it was probably a misunderstanding or an accident."

Eve was about to tell him the story of Walter pushing down the man in the grocery store but stopped as she heard someone talking in the background on the phone. Strider then quickly said, "Hey, I've got to go, but call me if you need me."

"Thanks, I will," she replied and hung up the phone.

On the drive back to the hotel she considered what her newfound knowledge could mean. Daisy's nomadic life could be indicative of a deeper instability. And what about Sterling? Although she hated to believe that Ben could have been right, maybe Sterling did struggle with issues of Post Traumatic Stress Disorder after serving a lifetime in the military. Was Millicent's boring life hiding something? Or Tom and Julie's? Of course, Eve's background check would probably reveal a similar mundaneness. She couldn't help but wonder if Walter's assault charge was dismissed due to the help of his powerful city council member daughter. And, although not a surprise to Eve, Ben's speeding tickets showed a disregard for laws and common decency.

She circled back to thoughts of Daisy. She hated to think it but... Daisy was widowed twice. Were her husbands' deaths due to natural causes? *Stop!* Eve reprimanded herself. *Do not pretend that this woman's tragic life is some sort of black widow true crime television special!* Then a far less empathetic inner voice said, *at least, not without some sort of proof.*

She was overanalyzing this information just like Strider knew she would. The only thing that Eve knew for sure was that it was very helpful to be on friendly terms with the local sheriff. She wondered if that had also been the case with Dirk's murderer. Perhaps that was why the death was quickly deemed accidental.

Chapter Twenty-Six

When she got back to the hotel, she found Ben sitting in the lobby playing a video game. This time, he chose not to wear headphones so Eve could hear the sounds of horror coming from his device. She walked up behind him and couldn't help but see the gruesome visual images that accompanied the sounds of gunshots and screaming. She forced herself to not let her disgust at his choice of entertainment deter her plan.

"Just who I wanted to see," she said happily as she put a hand on his shoulder.

Ben looked up with a surprised smile on his face. She thought he would like hearing that. Little did he know that her desire was to put him to work.

"I was wondering if you could you help me in my office scanning pictures today?"

"Sure," he said as he quickly turned off his game.

As he stood up, Eve read his T-shirt du jour: "Don't be ashamed of who you are. That's your parent's job."

Since Eve had just talked to her mother, she couldn't help but giggle at that one.

As she brought him into the office and showed him all

the pictures that needed to be scanned and in what order, she got the impression that Ben thought this was some sort of a date.

"So, you don't have kids?" Ben asked her.

"No," Eve replied concisely as she continued to organize the photos on the desk.

"Good. People get weird when they have kids," Ben said. "Once people become parents, they think that they're so smart and wise and stuff. I mean, yeah dude, you're smarter than your two-year-old, congratulations. And then the kids get older and sometimes smarter than their parents, but the parents still think they are the ones who know everything just because they're parents. Because parents know best, always and forever, no matter what. You know?"

"Um..." Eve wondered if Ben's t-shirt choice this morning prompted this particular topic or his current frustrations inspired the t-shirt choice.

"And people are always so excited to have a baby," Ben continued, "but when that baby grows up to be a teenager, they're all like— what? How did that happen? I didn't sign up for this. And then the kid becomes an adult and has— if you can believe it— their own personality. And again, a total shock to the parents. They're all, 'how could this person I made have it's own thoughts and opinions? I thought I was making a little human being that was going to be exactly like me, and think all the same things I do and do all the same things I do except only better,' you know?"

Eve laughed. "Yes, I have seen that. I have seen parents who say they want their child to be their own person, as long as that person is within the parameters of what they find acceptable."

"Yeah, and it's always 'do what I say, not what I do.' Like parents get a free pass to do a bunch of stupid stuff, make all the mistakes in the world, and do bad things but their kids are supposed to be perfect. Like, it's the kid's job to make up for their crap. So, if their kid is really good and smart and successful, then their slate is wiped clean, no matter what they did it the past."

"I'm sure parenting is just as complicated as is each child," said Eve. "I don't remember too much on parenting from my human behavior studies in college, but I do remember that overparenting can be just as detrimental as under-parenting. I'm sure it's hard to find that right balance. And like you said, all kids are different. Parents don't get to choose their children and vice versa. They can't change their children's personalities, but they can't change theirs either."

"Right?" Ben said, obviously not listening to Eve. "I mean, it's like it's a parent's job to be disappointed in their kids. I mean, what did they expect?"

"Well, I think your parents seem pretty nice, Ben," Eve said decisively.

Eve liked Tom and Julie and wasn't prepared to let Ben badmouth them. If that was indeed what he was doing. Eve couldn't really tell what was motivating his tirade. But if it was about his parents, she thought he should give them a break. The only bad parenting that she could see was that they had coddled him and enabled him to act like an irresponsible child well into adulthood.

She segued the conversation back to scanning pictures. "Speaking of kids... Look at how cute Millicent and Buck's little boy was."

Eve pulled out the stack of pictures from the 1980s and found one where little Christopher looked particularly adorable. In the photo, he was flanked by two women. As she showed the picture to an uninterested Ben, she realized that she knew the other woman in the photo with Millicent. Now that she had looked through all these old photos, she easily recognized a young Daisy.

She showed Ben what to do, and after she was satisfied that he had the hang of it, she left. She said she would be right back even though she had no intention to hurry. The point was to have Ben scan the pictures so she could have time to work on other things.

She checked in with her staff, making sure that everything and everyone was fine. As she made her way out to the horse pasture to check on her gigantic fur babies, she kept thinking of the picture of Daisy with Millicent and Christopher.

She was happy to find Tom in the stables taking his emergency horse care duties very seriously. She was even happier to find Millicent there talking to Tom. After verifying with Tom that he knew where everything was and had everything he needed, Eve wanted to see what Tom had to say about his son. The gore of the video game he had been playing disturbed her more than a little. She couldn't help but wonder if it was a sign that Ben was possibly dangerous.

"So," she began awkwardly, "Ben was playing a pretty violent video game this morning. Is that what he's always playing? Shooting and killing?"

"I hate that brain-rot," interjected Millicent. "It's no wonder the youth of today have no morals or manners."

Tom nodded at Millicent and looked at Eve thoughtfully. "I know, I find those games concerning also. But a lot of people play them and enjoy them. In fact, I've read that numerous studies have shown no link between playing those games and aggressive behavior."

"Yes, I suppose that there could be an argument that it actually quells the violent urge by acting out fictional scenarios," Eve contemplated. "But I still don't like them."

"I understand," Tom said, "but rest assured, my son is a lover, not a fighter. He takes after me in that respect." Tom winked at Eve and Millicent before he meandered out to the pasture. As she watched Tom walk away, she wondered if that was true. *Is he really a lover and not a fighter?* The picture of him with the black eye she found earlier certainly looked like the face of a fighter.

Then Eve's thoughts returned to another photograph: the picture she had seen more recently. She jumped at the chance to question Millicent about it while they were alone. "I was just looking through some of your photos and I noticed a picture of Daisy with you and Christopher."

"So?" Millicent said with a sideways glance.

"So... Daisy didn't work here then."

"She used to come visit sometimes," Millicent said and then briskly walked away before Eve could ask any follow up questions.

Eve wondered if Millicent's behavior was suspicious. Perhaps it was just her natural disregard for pleasantries.

On her way back to the hotel Eve saw Daisy sitting at the side of the pool with her feet dangling in the water. She veered off course and joined her.

"That looks nice and refreshing," said Eve.

"It's lovely. Come join me. You need to detoxify your thoughts."

"I do?"

"Everyone does."

"Why not?" Eve said. She quickly took off her shoes and rolled up her pant legs. "How are you doing, Daisy?" she asked as she sat beside her and dunked her feet in the water.

"Glorious. It's nice to be back here," replied Daisy as she peered up at the sky. "What an amazing display the heavens are putting on for us today."

Eve joined her companion in lifting her gaze upwards to appreciate the majesty above.

"Clouds are the ever-changing art exhibit in the sky," said Daisy. "Sometimes it's art that you've seen before that doesn't do anything for you. But sometimes it's art that speaks to your soul and its beauty and intensity just blows you away."

"Wow, lovely," Eve said in awe of the moment. "I can't believe I didn't notice it before. It's really spectacular right now. So many colors, and so many different kinds of clouds. Do you know the different types?"

"No, I prefer to enjoy the art of the clouds without concerning my brain with the science of clouds. But I do remember that Cirrus clouds are the wispy ones that look like brush strokes."

After some time soaking in the exceptional beauty and power of nature, Eve said, "I'm glad you made it to the reunion, Daisy. I was wondering if I could schedule you for a history interview tomorrow."

"Oh, I'm sure I have nothing interesting to tell you about the hotel. I just peeled potatoes."

"I'm sure there is plenty that you can tell me. Like, what was your favorite meal that Millicent made?"

"Oh, the meatloaf. She made amazing meatloaf. Nobody makes that anymore, do they?"

"See? That's great information. Maybe I can get her meatloaf recipe and feature it on our menu as a tribute to the original hotel."

"You can call it Millicent's Meatloaf!" Daisy suggested excitedly.

"Perfect! I would love that! See, you have already helped me."

"Okay, what else do you want to know?"

"Um… well, I thought it was interesting to hear that you left the hotel shortly after Annabelle went off to boarding school. Everyone else here only left after the hotel had to be closed due to the construction of the interstate that by-passed this section of Route 66. Why did you leave earlier?"

"Family emergency."

"Sorry to hear that." Eve remained quiet after that, not wanting to pry. If Daisy wanted to elaborate, she could.

After a minute of silence, Daisy mumbled, "I went to live with family… in a town called What Cheer. I always said — What cheer can be found in a town named What Cheer."

"I've heard of that town. Is it as cute as the name?" Eve asked kindly.

Daisy nodded and smiled. "When do you want to do my history interview?" she asked.

They made plans to do Daisy's history interview sometime in the late morning tomorrow, before or after Millicent's.

"Speaking of Millicent… she told me that you used to come visit sometimes after you stopped working here."

"Yes."

"Did other ex-employees come out and visit also?"

"No, I don't think so."

"You and Millicent were friends?"

"She was good to me. She's not as mean as she acts."

Eve opened her mouth to question the wording of Daisy's statement but thought better of it. She allowed herself a little time to relax with her most eccentric guest. Even though Daisy was a bit odd, she had a pleasant, easy energy. She was one of those people that you could share a comfortable silence with. After a short while, Eve started to feel guilty that she was relaxing by the pool while Ben was doing her scanning work for her. She excused herself and headed back to the hotel.

When she returned to the office, she expected to find Ben perturbed at being abandoned for so long. Instead, she was greeted with a genuine smile.

"Look," he said as he handed her a photograph.

It was a picture of Julie on a horse with Tom standing next to her. Eve admired how pretty Julie was and how obviously smitten Tom was as he stared up at Julie. It was so adorable, so romantic.

"Very cute," said Eve.

"I know," agreed Ben.

Eve looked at the back of the photo. It was unmarked which meant it was one of the photos Sterling just gave her. "Go show your dad," she suggested as she held out the photo. "I think he's still out in the horse pasture or the stables."

Eve watched a happy Ben walk out of the office. She supposed seeing his parents as young people reminded him that they were human beings, not just the rule enforcing authority figures in his life.

Eve looked to see how much scanning Ben had accomplished in her absence. Certainly not as much as she would have hoped. She suspected he had been too busy looking at the pictures to scan them. She looked through the next few photos to see if there were any more of Tom and Julie to show Ben on his return. She sifted through the photos and thought she had found another cute one of the two of them at the shooting range. Julie was in the middle of a shooting lesson with the arms of a young man wrapped around her showing her how to hold a rifle. But on closer inspection, Eve realized that the young man was not Tom, it was Dirk.

Chapter Twenty-Seven

Gil sat in one of the guest chairs in the office for his history interview.

"You're not going to put me to work scanning pictures are you? Ben said you were a stern taskmaster," Gil joked.

"Ben's work ethic could use a little toughening up," replied Eve.

"Oh, give him a break. He's a good kid."

Eve had a lot of things she wanted to talk about with Gil, but Ben was not one of them. First, she really did want to complete Gil's history interview. She started recording and she asked him all about his work in the hotel kitchen: the dishes they prepared, what it was like working with Millicent, and much more. After she had covered all the questions on her list, she seamlessly switched subjects.

"And everything at the hospital was okay?" Eve asked nonchalantly.

"Yeah, like I said, Wes didn't even need stitches. He's fine. Wes's girlfriend June is so cute. She was so worried. She was waiting for him at the entrance of her ranch. She was pacing back and forth when we pulled up. When

Wes got out the car, she ran up to him and — "

A fevered knocking on the office door stopped Gil talking.

"Come in," called Eve.

"Sorry," said Roxie as she poked her head in. "You need to come out here."

Gil remained in the office while Roxie led Eve to the dining room and pointed to the floor.

"I'll clean it up, but I just wanted you to see it first," said Roxie.

The offending mess was the broken glass of the picture frame with the photo featuring Dirk. Had it fallen or had someone smashed it on the floor? It appeared to be the latter.

"When did this happen? I didn't hear anything," said Eve.

"I don't know. I just found it right now," said Roxie.

Daisy walked in through the back door and came upon the scene of the broken picture frame. "Ernest!" she gasped.

Eve had had enough of this nonsense. "Daisy, there is no Ernest! Millicent admitted that she made him up."

"That doesn't mean he doesn't exist," Daisy countered.

"Yes, it does! That's how fiction works."

"Well, maybe his name isn't Ernest but there is a ghost here, a ghost that punishes the wicked. I know." After her assured statement, Daisy walked into the lobby.

"Do you think it was a ghost?" Eve asked Roxie.

"I don't know," said Roxie with a shrug of her shoulders. "That would be cool, I guess. People like haunted hotels, I think. Maybe we'll get more business if we have a ghost. So, do you want me to put the picture in a new frame? I think we have some more down in the basement."

"No. I think it's best if we don't put this photo back up. I'll find a replacement later. Just throw away the frame and put the photo down in the basement for now. Thanks, Roxie."

Eve made her way back to the office to finish her conversation with Gil, but he had left. As she sat back down, she caught sight of the Route 66 Ranch Hotel Grand Opening flyer she had put on her wall. It was only a week away. Was she going to be prepared? Why did she plan these two events so close together? And was the grand opening going to be grand enough? Should she have planned more events, more activities? Perhaps she should have a cow plop. Yes! That would be a fun tradition to bring back to the property. Eve wondered if Wes's girlfriend, June, could borrow a cow from her boss.

Then it hit her — June! Gil dropped off Wes at the entrance to June's ranch. Earlier, Eve had determined that the 54 miles that had been driven on her car was a roundtrip to Sandmat, but if Gil took Wes out to June's, that couldn't be the case, the mileage would have been higher. So, where had Gil taken Wes before taking her to June's?

Unable to come up with an answer to her question, Eve decided to use her time before her next history interview to work on something she knew she could actually accomplish. She wanted to review the footage from last night's Storytime to make sure the video had turned out, especially the audio. She watched a little, then skipped to the next person and listened making sure the audio for that particular story sounded good. She repeated this until she was at the end and satisfied that the camera had successfully captured everyone's stories. She rewatched Daisy talking about Ernest and remembered Daisy's haunting words, "The people here should watch out." Eve shivered despite the fact that, even if she believed in ghosts, which she did not, she knew Ernest had been admittedly fabricated.

She became distracted by a pile of mail she hadn't yet opened. As she sorted through the collection of advertisements and bills, she began to hear strange noises. She chastised her imagination for playing into Daisy's ghost obsession. There wasn't anything there, she told herself.

While opening a bill with her antique letter opener she suddenly knew that she was definitely hearing voices — eerie voices that sounded close and distant at the same time. She held the letter opener a little tighter. These strange noises could not simply be explained away by the sounds of people in another room. She stopped breathing and listened to the indistinct voices that somehow surrounded her.

She slowly began to survey the room for signs of an explanation. She finally let out a relieved gasp. The video was still playing! She had forgotten the video footage was playing just as she had forgotten that she had left the camera on last night. All this talk of a haunted hotel was making her jumpy. As she laughed at herself, she took a deep calming breath and tried to make out what the voices on the video were saying and to whom they belonged.

One question was quickly answered as Sterling meandered into the frame.

Sterling was looking off camera, obviously in the middle of a conversation with someone, and quietly but clearly said, "I'll stay quiet about it if you do." After some more muffled voice sounds that Eve could not discern, Sterling said, "Yes. I'll take care of it." He then walked off. There was nothing more of interest on the video.

Eve watched it again trying to figure out who Sterling was talking to but couldn't. She couldn't even determine if the disembodied voice off-camera was a man or woman. Then she watched it again for any clue as to what Sterling meant. Was this concerning Dirk's murder or Wes getting shot? Or did someone spill red wine on a white tablecloth? But after watching it for a third time, Eve conceded that there were no clues to determine the subject matter. It was yet another mystery to add to her list.

A knock on the office door made her jump and she quickly turned off the Storytime footage to hide her inadvertent spying before she called out, "Come in!"

The door opened revealing the subject of her next history interview, Tom. He must had heard the nervousness in her voice because he gave her a concerned look as he entered. "Are you ready for me? I can come back later if you need."

"No, I'm ready," said Eve quickly. "Or rather, I will be. Just give me a second." She sifted through the papers on her desk to find her interview questions for Tom. "Go ahead and have a seat."

Tom was the perfect interview subject. He had a great memory and answered every question with wonderful details that satisfied many of Eve's questions about the former trail riding operation at the Arizona Sunset Ranch Hotel. He even remembered dates of events and the names of almost all the employees he had worked with. And he didn't just answer the questions with one-word answers, they all were accompanied with a charming story.

But Tom's amazing memory seemed to falter when asked about his black eye.

"Black eye?" he asked.

"Yes," Eve explained, "I have a picture here somewhere." She pretended to sift through the box of photos on the floor, although she had set it on top for this occasion. "Here it is," she said and set it down on the desk in front of him.

"Oh, I don't remember that," Tom said.

"Earlier, you told me that you were a lover, not a fighter, but you sure look like a fighter in this picture," she said lightheartedly.

"Oh no, definitely not a fighter," he said as he stared at the picture. "How was I ever that young?"

"You don't remember how you got the black eye?" Eve persisted.

"I think I got bucked off a horse," he said as he slowly started nodding his head. "But who knows when that happened."

"It was the summer of '77, shortly before Annabelle left for boarding school. I know because you have the same black eye in this picture." Eve quickly grabbed the group picture from the top of the pile, this time foregoing the pretense of looking for it. She set it next to the other photograph.

"Oh yes, it looks like it was," Tom said with a smile. "I looked so tough! I remember that day. I looked tough and little Annabelle was trying to act tough. She was trying so hard to hide her nervousness. Leaving home at that age is traumatic. The experience definitely changed her. She left a little girl and came back a young woman. I actually spent more time with her after that. When she would come back home she always wanted to ride horses. Sometimes she would bring friends from school, and she liked to show off all her horses and her exceptional riding skills. I was happy to help her. After all, horses are very important to teenage girls."

Eve's mind wandered. She thought how impressed she would have been at that age if one of her friends had access to a team of horses. As Tom thanked her for the interview and made a graceful exit, Eve's mind returned to the present. She first thought how, now as an adult, she was impressed with the skillful way Tom had just changed the subject and disappeared. And then she thought how his retreating figure reminded her of Gil — how she had mistaken Gil for Tom. She couldn't help but wonder: did the shooter do the same?

Chapter Twenty-Eight

Wes called and let Eve know that June had dropped him off at his cabin. He would be back to work in the morning. She again asked him about his well-being, and he again assured her that he was fine. He mentioned that after the shooting he saw the wreckage of a rollover car accident (she assumed it was the same one that Sheriff Strider had responded to that day) and said that it really put things into perspective. It forced him to realize how truly lucky he was.

She was so happy he was okay, and that things would get back to normal soon. But after the phone call, her thoughts once again returned to the missing miles on her odometer. After musing on the possibilities all afternoon, she was pretty sure she had figured it out. And now, after what Wes just said, she was almost positive. Thirty miles roundtrip one direction and then twenty-four miles roundtrip in the other direction would equal the mysterious fifty-four miles that had been driven.

She wanted to talk to Gil about it privately before dinner. She found him on the veranda reading a magazine. She sat down next to him.

She decided to be direct this time. "Gil, where did you take Wes? I know you didn't take him to the hospital."

Gil took a deep breath before asking, "Did Wes tell you?"

"No. That would have been nice, but no. For some reason, he did not. He did mention that you saw the aftermath of that rollover accident that happened on the way to Sandmat. A scene you would not have been driving by if you went to the hospital and back. But I already knew you didn't go to the hospital. The mileage on my car didn't add up."

Gil looked down sheepishly.

"Well, I didn't want to take Wes to the hospital with a gunshot wound," he said. "I didn't want them to call the cops and open an investigation."

"So where did you take him? Dr. Nadar's? If you drove out to Naiya's place and then out to June's ranch, that would account for the mileage on my odometer."

"Wow, yes, that's exactly what I did. You figured that out just from your odometer?"

"That, and the Midas touch. That wet spot on your pants was similar to the one I had received from Midas when I was visiting Naiya's property."

"Hey, I thought my spilled iced tea story was pretty good."

"Gil, I know you think Wes's getting shot was an accident. Maybe it was. I'm not going to argue with you about that again. But I would really appreciate it if you would tell me who you think killed Dirk. I realize that you don't know for sure. I'm not going to start a lynch mob with the information. I just need to know." She looked at him imploringly. "Please," she added.

He looked at her for a full minute before speaking.

"Well, okay," he finally said. "At the time— and remember I was young and stupid— but at the time, I was sure it was Buck. I had overheard an argument between the two of them. Buck said, 'If I find out the missing cattle

160

have anything to do with you, I will kill you.' I was frightened that they were going to see me and I snuck off. The next time I saw Dirk he was covered in bruises. I assumed the argument turned into a beating after I left. Then, next thing I knew, I heard a rumor that Dirk was dead. It was very hush, hush. The company line was that it was an accident and no more was to be spoken of it. Buck was my boss's husband. I wasn't about to breathe a word about what I had overheard that day. I didn't want to lose my job and, well, honestly, Buck scared me. But, like I said, I was young. I didn't really know Buck and I didn't know what was going on behind the scenes around here."

"Dirk was covered in bruises when he was found shot dead?"

"Yes."

"Certainly, that would point to the death being intentional. But the sheriff didn't investigate?"

"I guess not. It was a different time and Sheriff Weed was ready to retire. He was probably just going through the motions at that point. Plus, this was a respectable place. If someone told him that a guest who was long gone accidentally killed Dirk, there was no reason for him to not believe it."

Julie walked out of the dining room door and joined them on the veranda. "Sorry to interrupt, but Annabelle just told me that she is going to stay with her father in his suite tonight and asked if they could have dinner taken to them."

"I'll do it," Gil said as he jumped up from his seat.

"You don't have to do that," said Eve.

"Well, I think that room service duty is the least I can do for being a thorn in your side since I have been here. I'll see what they would like from tonight's menu." He walked inside.

"Julie, come sit with me," suggested Eve in a friendly manner.

"Sure, it's beautiful out here."

After Julie sat, they engaged in some pleasantries about the beauty of the red rock cliffs that bordered the north side of the property and some other small talk before Eve broached her intended subject.

"So...," she finally began, "I saw some pictures of you and Dirk together." Technically it was only one picture, but she wanted to trick Julie into talking. She waited to see how Julie would respond to the proof that she had lied.

Julie craned her neck in both directions, surveying the area to make sure they were alone. In a hushed voice she said, "Yes, I knew him."

"Why did you lie?"

"Shame. Denial."

"So, you knew him well?"

"Too well. He was cute— really cute— and I was young. I can't believe how stupid I was back then. He wasn't nice to me, not at all, but I was so inexperienced, I didn't know any better." Julie looked around again to make sure no one was around. "Eventually he talked me into sleeping with him and I felt so used. I was humiliated when he immediately tossed me aside. He was so mean. He said I wasn't pretty enough for him and that I was too old for him. I was so ashamed. I was sick about it. I tried to hide that I had ever even talked to him."

"I'm starting to understand why no one seemed to care too much about his death."

"From that day forward, I pretended that I never knew him. In fact, I have never told Tom that I had anything to do with Dirk."

"He knows."

"He does?"

"He made a jealous sounding comment that you liked Dirk."

"Oh," Julie said as she stared out into the distance. "He's never mentioned it. We've never talked about it. If

I'm being honest, I thought he might have known, but we've never talked about it. I — " Julie stopped talking when she heard the dining room door open.

Ben peeked his head out of the door and said, "Eve, they want you in the kitchen."

Eve went to the kitchen and fielded a few questions about dinner arrangements. While she was there, she offered to help Esperanza and Roxie with last minute preparations for dinner.

"So, has that guy asked you out on a date yet?" Roxie asked Eve teasingly.

"Who, Ben? Thankfully, no. I hope he doesn't. That would be awkward. I hate turning down a guy. It's the worst."

"You could always say yes," suggested Esperanza.

"Not in a million years would I go out with Ben," whispered Eve.

"Oh, he's not that bad. He actually reminds me of Gil's son," said Esperanza.

"I was wondering why Gil seemed to have a soft spot for Ben," Eve said mindlessly as she took some rolls out of the oven.

The women continued to work in silence as Eve started to wonder if Gil actually saw Ben shoot Wes. Perhaps that was why Gil was so adamant that it was an accident. Ben reminded Gil of his own son and he naturally felt an obligation to protect the ne'er-do-well. But what if it wasn't an accident? What if Ben was a crazy person who was trying to shoot Wes out of jealousy? Or what if he was trying to actually shoot Gil to protect one or both of his parents because he knew, or thought, one of them murdered Dirk?

"All I know," Roxie said, interrupting Eve's thoughts, "is that he needs to learn how to use his 'do not disturb' sign."

"Why?" asked Esperanza.

"Because, yesterday when I was making the beds in

the rooms, I thought he wasn't in his room, but he was. I knocked and everything -- just in case -- but when I went in, he was laying on the bed. I was so embarrassed. I mean, what if he was naked or something?"

"Didn't he hear you knock?"

"No, he had his headphones on, and he was faced the other way, so he didn't even see that I opened the door. But, come on. Use the sign, dude. I hope other people are smart enough to do that. I don't want to be walking in on people. His was the last room I did, and no one was in any of the other rooms, so I totally wasn't expecting it."

"Was that right before you came down to the kitchen yesterday? Is that why you were blushing?" Eve asked.

"Yes. It was embarrassing!"

Eve's deduction that Ben shot Wes was dashed. If Roxie had walked in on Ben yesterday morning, that would have been right before Eve drove out to see Gil and Wes. There was no way that he could have made it out to the old shooting range in time.

"Roxie, why didn't you tell me this?" Eve asked. "I've been thinking this whole time that Ben might have been the one who shot Wes!"

"I didn't know!" Roxie squealed.

"In Roxie's defense," Esperanza said calmly, "when you told us about the shooting, you did say that you thought it was one of the old hotel employees who did it and Ben isn't one of them."

"You're right." Eve said. "I'm sorry, Roxie. At least, now I know Ben didn't do it."

Between this information and the mounting lies that seemed to surround Dirk's death, Eve couldn't help but think that her original thought had merit. Perhaps the two shootings were connected. Because if Ben didn't shoot at Wes and Gil, that meant it was definitely someone who had been here when Dirk was murdered.

Chapter Twenty-Nine

Eve and Roxie had just finished delivering the last of the food to the dinner buffet set on the bar in the dining room. They were heading back into the kitchen to make sure they didn't miss anything when Sterling walked down the stairs to the lobby carrying his ever-present duffel bag.

"Perfect timing. Dinner's ready," Eve announced.

"I was just going to go out –" he replied, nodding towards the front door.

"No, come on," said Roxie. "Everything is nice and hot right now. Come on." Roxie went over to him and wrapped her arm through his and led him to the dining room. Eve couldn't help but inwardly laugh again at Roxie's inconsistent personality. She was so embarrassed to have walked in on Ben when he was completely dressed, and yet she was completely at ease physically pulling this intimidating stranger into the other room.

Daisy was the last to arrive to dinner. She was wearing even more fanciful layers of gauzy material than usual. As she walked in, she surveyed the available seat options and quickly made her choice to sit next to Sterling.

Dinner was pleasant despite the lack of Annabelle's joyful presence that always seemed to help unify the group. The main topic of conversation was when the hotel closed down due to the construction of the interstate.

"It was so sad that the hotel had to close and we all had to leave," said Julie.

"Not for me!" countered Millicent. "We adopted Christopher that spring. I had a baby less than a year old. I was exhausted. The hotel closing couldn't have come at a better time for me. Only having to cook for the remaining staff and the ranch workers was like a vacation."

"Well, it was sad for the rest of us," Tom said.

"I thought you stayed on to take care of the horses," Eve said.

"I did but it was sad seeing everyone else go," Tom explained. It was depressing. It was the end of year, it was cold and dismal, and everyone was distraught about what their future held. And then everyone left for the holidays and never came back. It was lonely. The girl I liked was gone," he said as looked at Julie. "My friend left," he said as he looked at Sterling. Then Tom let out a loud laugh. "I was sure a sensitive lad, wasn't I? I should have written a poem about it!"

After dinner, Ramon, Esperanza, Loretta and Roxie all went home to their cabins. Eve had assured them that she alone could take care of the guests during dessert and after-dinner drinks. They were all reluctant to leave Eve until Gil, professional restauranteur, promised them he would help. Gil was a natural host and always ready to lend a hand.

Everyone had clustered in small groups for quiet conversations. Julie and Millicent, Gil and Ben, and Tom, Sterling, and Daisy. Eve was happy to have the distraction of being in charge, making sure that her guests were happy and well provided for the rest of the evening. Refilling coffee mugs, mixing cocktails, and clearing dessert plates took her mind off other matters. Everyone seemed in good spirits with that satisfied relaxation that follows a good meal. Eve felt a good energy emanating from the room until suddenly, there was no energy at all. The lights went out and the room plunged into complete darkness.

"Oh no!"

"I can't see a thing."

"Why did the power go off?"

"A storm I guess."

"But it's not even raining."

"Get your phone."

"I left it upstairs."

"Me too."

"Mine just died!"

"Please, don't worry!" Eve said loudly over all the voices talking at once. "The power often comes right back on." Eve reached for her cell phone only to realize she didn't have it on her. She must have misplaced it as she often did.

Despite her suggestion to not worry, Eve could hear the sounds of chairs moving and people getting up and moving around. The nervousness that had taken over the room was affecting Eve. She too started to worry. People act erratically during blackouts. A bright flash of lightning illuminated the room for a moment. Eve looked for Gil but only saw Tom, who appeared to be walking towards the bar. A moment later, the accompanying thunderclap shook the building. Someone jumped and bumped into Eve, probably Ben she thought, and someone else shrieked, probably Julie she thought.

Although she was telling the truth about the lights often coming right back on, she knew that sometimes they stayed off for hours. She decided she better make her way towards the cabinet in the lobby where she kept all the battery operated lanterns. She groped her way along the walls. She thought she heard a door open and close. She quickly grabbed a lantern and turned it on. As she walked back to the dining room, the lights came back, temporarily blinding her. She blinked a few times and entered the dining room.

"It never fails, as soon as I get a —" She stopped talking once she realized everyone was suspiciously still and quiet. Eve scanned the room for Gil, but he wasn't there. She started to panic. "Where's Gil?"

Daisy looked at Eve and said, "Ernest."

"What? No. Gil. Where's Gil?"

A voice behind her said, "I'm here. I was looking, well— feeling, for candles in the kitchen."

Relief washed over Eve as she turned to verify that it was Gil. Gil was fine. Everything was fine. She returned her gaze to the rest of the group in the dining room and realized they were all still acting peculiar and were all looking towards the west side of the room. Eve took another step forward so that she could see what was captivating everyone's attention. Gil's missing rifle was laying on top of the bar.

"Ernest," Daisy repeated softly.

As Eve stared at the rifle in a daze, the storm finally hit the hotel. The strong wind propelled the sheets of rain onto the building in a deafening roar.

Eve raised her voice to make sure everyone could hear her over the violent storm. "Is anyone going to admit to putting that there?" Only silence followed. "I didn't think so. I suggest everyone go to their rooms immediately before the power goes off again."

Everyone just kept staring at the rifle.

Eve marched over to the bar, picked up the rifle and said, "I'll take this!" As she grabbed the rifle, the room plunged into darkness once again. Luckily, she hadn't turned off her lantern. "Everyone, follow me," she ordered.

She led them to the cabinet of lanterns. She felt ridiculous as she rationed out lanterns with one hand while holding a rifle in the other. There were just enough lanterns for every person there.

"Tom and I can share," said Julie. "I'll bring this one to Annabelle."

"I'll do it," said Eve as she took the lantern from Julie. "I'd like to check in with her and Walter."

Eve watched the guests walk up the stairs, their lanterns creating creepy dancing shadows as they moved.

Gil had stayed behind and followed Eve up to Walter's suite. Eve gently knocked on the door and said, "Annabelle? Are you in there? It's Eve."

Annabelle opened the door. Eve couldn't tell if it was due to the way the light of the lantern was hitting her face, but Annabelle looked ghastly. She looked like she had seen a ghost.

"Are you okay?" Eve asked instinctually.

"Um… yes. I just didn't want to leave my dad."

"I brought a lantern for you. This happens occasionally during monsoon season. Nothing to worry about. Hopefully the power will come on soon for the sake of all the food in the refrigerator," Eve said lightheartedly in an attempt to ease Annabelle's obvious discomfort.

"Okay, thanks," Annabelle said distractedly as she took the lantern and closed the door.

Eve wondered if Annabelle was simply afraid of the dark. She knew it was an affliction some people struggled with their entire lives.

"Do you need anything else?" Gil asked.

Eve jumped. She had completely forgotten he was behind her. Maybe she was a little more afraid of the dark than she admitted to herself.

She looked at Gil somberly as she said, "Just make sure you lock your door."

Chapter Thirty

That night, Eve had a recurring dream in which she was at a magic show where the magician made a rifle disappear and reappear over and over again. She tried to figure out who the magician was but could not see a face. She was filled with dread every time the rifle disappeared. And she was equally distraught every time the rifle reappeared. She wanted to make her way towards the stage, to stop the show, to pull the magician from the shadows to reveal his or her identity. But she couldn't do any of those things. She couldn't move. She felt useless.

It was a classic frustration dream. But finally, she was rewarded. Her frustration was relieved. She saw the magician's face. He walked into the disappearing box and turned around with a flourish. The magician was Gil. He closed the door, locking himself in the box. A moment later it opened by itself. He was gone. Gil had disappeared.

Eve woke up in a panic. The dream seemed important. Her half-asleep mind struggled to figure out why. As the connection to her subconscious slowly lessened, she lost her understanding of the dream. Once the fog of sleep had completely lifted, she decided she was being ridiculous, it was just a nonsensical dream. It was 4:30 in the morning and she had no interest in returning to that pointless magic show dream. She might as well stay awake.

She sat up and turned on the bedside lamp. *The light came on!* Good, the power outage was over. She automatically reached for the box of her great aunt's diaries.

She felt like taking a break from pouring over Genevieve's diaries of the late seventies, looking for clues about Dirk's murder. She chose a diary from 1958 instead. But as she began to read, she found herself still speed reading through the parts that didn't involve the ranch. As she saw the word 'Arizona' she slowed down to absorb the text.

March 12, 1958

It's a beautiful, sunny late winter day in Arizona. I'm fairly certain the east coast is steeped in an icy fog at the moment. I cannot help but feel that I'm in paradise after spending a relaxing day on horseback with the Arizona sunshine warming my face and my spirits.

I believe I have a new favorite horse to ride. He is a new acquisition but an older horse. He is so mild mannered and seems to know where I want to turn before I do myself. I think he may be the perfect horse, other than his name. His name is dreadful. I have no idea who named the creature, but he must have thought himself quite the comedian naming such a gentle soul "The Killer."

The Killer was the name of a horse! That was what Walter was referring to when he was staring out at the empty horse pasture.

Her delight at having one small mystery solved

dissipated quickly as she caught sight of Gil's rifle propped up in the corner of her room. As she stared at it, her thoughts returned to the possible connection of Dirk's murder and Wes's shooting. She then thought of the two separate incidents. She imagined each of her guests shooting Dirk, and then visualized each of them shooting Wes. What made sense? Who made sense?

A swirl of recent memories made her dizzy: Millicent saying she would do anything for her late husband; Gil's ill-timed announcement that he knew who killed Dirk; Julie lying about knowing Dirk; Daisy's insistence that there was a spirit here who punished the wicked; Tom's black eye; Sterling saying that Dirk was not worth remembering; Walter talking about taking out the trash and Annabelle's shooting competitions.

Eve once again considered the possibility that Walter knew who killed Dirk. Suddenly, it occurred to her that if Walter did know the truth, he could be in danger. This was a suspicion that she would keep to herself. She wouldn't want to suggest to the murderer that Walter was a possible threat. But in his current state of mind, he could say anything to anyone. Eve was happy that Annabelle had kept him safely away from the others last night.

Now that her mind was once again fully fixated on the shootings, she wanted to know everything she could about the time when Dirk was murdered. She had already read all of Genevieve's diary entries from around that time in 1977. Did she have any other resources to mine for information? She remembered the letter Genevieve had written to Minna in on August 21st of 1977. The other day, Eve had read only half of it and set it aside.

She picked it up and began reading in the middle of the letter, where she had left off.

But it is not all fun and relaxation here at the moment. I have been busy making phone calls trying to get a last-minute placement in a boarding school for the caretakers' daughter. I believe, in the past, I have told you of Walter and Constance's daughter, Annabelle. Mr. Thorton asked me to make the arrangements and it is proving to be quite a challenge finding an opening at this late stage. But I am hopeful that with Mr. Thorton's connections we will be able to accomplish it soon. Then I can truly take a break from work!

I hope you are enjoying the freedom of youth. I wish I had. I was perhaps too enthusiastic to mature and to start a career. I wish I had spent more time being young. It is not something to which one can return.

Love always,
Your Aunt Genevieve

Eve didn't know what she had expected to find in that last half of the letter. Had she expected Genevieve to write "P.S. I found out that --- murdered Dirk."? That would have been nice.

Eve set down the letter and got in the shower to get ready for her day. As she did so, she thought about the contents of the letter.

First, she giggled to herself wondering if perhaps her mother took this letter to heart. In a way, Eve's mother, Minna, never really matured and she was never interested in starting a career. She always worked but she never took any job too seriously. She made it her life's mission to enjoy her youth, even after it was gone. Eve reflected on how the two most important role models of her life while she was growing up, her mother and her great aunt, were very different people. *And I picked up the best qualities from both of them... And that's why I'm perfect!*

But then, Eve's thoughts returned to what the letter had revealed about that summer of 1977. Annabelle's being sent off to boarding school was a last-minute event. *That is interesting... very interesting*, thought Eve. And her thoughts were once again fixated on the mysterious shootings.

Chapter Thirty-One

Once dressed and ready for her day, Eve was filled with a determination to find out the truth before her guests left tomorrow. She wanted to know who shot Wes and why, and who shot Dirk and why. She was certain that at the very least Dirk's death had been an intentional murder. Perhaps it wasn't premeditated but Eve was sure that someone had wanted him dead. He was too hated by everyone for his murder to be accidental. In fact, more than one person wanted him gone, but who hated him enough to kill?

But how was she going to do it? She supposed she could get everyone together and throw a tantrum until everyone honestly answered her questions. Perhaps it was not the most sophisticated of solutions, but the idea of throwing a good old-fashioned tantrum sounded therapeutic. Or should she call Sheriff Strider? Should she have him threaten to arrest them all unless they told the truth? The sheriff had been very accommodating up until now, but Eve didn't think he would do that for her. Perhaps he could come and throw a good old-fashioned tantrum on her behalf. Even in her prickly mood, the thought of that ridiculous suggestion made her smile briefly.

She grumpily marched into the kitchen to find her employees having their coffee and breakfast at the butcher block table and benches Eve had recently purchased. It made the large kitchen feel homier. Seeing her new work family gathered around for a meal made Eve's irritability vanish.

Esperanza got up to pour Eve the last of the coffee and make another pot. As she did, she said happily, "Wes is back to work today. That's good news."

"Where is he?" Eve asked.

"Oh, you know the early schedule he keeps. He was here finishing his coffee and on his way out the door when we arrived," replied Esperanza.

"He said he's taking Tempest out for a ride so she gets more used to it here," said Loretta.

"Did he look okay?" asked Eve.

"Never better," replied Esperanza.

"Good, thanks."

"So, Eve," began Loretta. "You ever find out what happened? Who shot Wes? You been so busy, I ain't seen to you."

Eve shook her head.

"I bet it's the scary guy. As soon as I saw him, I knew there was something wrong about him," Loretta said to the group.

"Sterling?" Ramon asked.

Loretta nodded. "Yeah, that one."

"I like Sterling," said Ramon. "I have had some truly pleasant and fascinating conversations with him. Yesterday he was telling me that we live in an "IBA" which is an Important Bird Area. Apparently, this is an extremely important breeding and migration area for birds, especially raptors like eagles and hawks. There have been sixteen different species of raptors reported being spotted in our area including Prairie Falcons, Red-

Tailed Hawks, Great-Horned Owls, Burrowing—"

"Oh no! There's two of them now!" Eve joked.

"Don't worry, Eve," Esperanza said with a smile to her husband. "Next week, he'll be fascinated by something new."

Ramon's eyes twinkled as he cutely replied, "Probably." He turned his attention back to Eve. "In all seriousness, Sterling does not strike me as a man who would wildly start shooting a gun with no regard to his surroundings."

Eve nodded and said, "I really have no idea who did it. They say ignorance is bliss, but not for me. Ignorance drives me up the wall. I feel like I'm just as in the dark as before. Speaking of 'in the dark'… I take it your power went off at the cabins last night too?"

"Yes, it was so fun," said Roxie. "I spent all night scaring Mom with ghost stories about Ernest."

"You annoyed me all night with ghost stories," said Loretta.

"That's what made it fun!" Roxie laughed as the smile Loretta was trying to hide finally revealed itself.

"Well, it was not fun here," said Eve. "I think we need to get a generator like you so wisely suggested before, Ramon. Can you look into that for me?"

"Certainly," he responded.

"I never again want to have a hotel full of guests left in the dark."

"And believe me, you also never want a kitchen full of rotting food," said Esperanza.

The remark reminded Eve of her comment to Annabelle last night and how absolutely horrible and stressed Annabelle had looked. She realized that she had been nervously chewing her fingernails during their brief encounter as she had seen her do earlier, but Eve remembered that last night, Annabelle had practically no fingernails left. Her stress was coming to a head. Perhaps Eve should go have a conversation with her and see if there was anything she could do to help. Annabelle must be having an increasingly difficult time being her father's caretaker. Perhaps it would help to have someone tell her that she needn't be solely responsible for taking care of her father. Sometimes just hearing an outsider's perspective helped someone accept the reality of a situation.

After another cup of coffee and a few nibbles on a breakfast roll, Eve headed upstairs to Annabelle's room. She knocked but there was no answer. She then knocked on Walter's connecting suite. As she knocked, the door creaked open. She was concerned. She opened the door slowly and peeked in. No sign of Walter. She walked into the room a little farther. The connecting door to Annabelle's room was open. Eve could hear the sound of water running from that direction. Annabelle was most likely taking a shower, but where was Walter? And why did it appear that all of their luggage was packed and ready to go? Everyone was supposed to be staying another night. But Eve forced herself to focus on the most pressing issue, which was the location of Walter. She made sure he wasn't in Annabelle's room, the bathroom, or the balcony before she allowed her panic to set in.

She hurried downstairs and enlisted her employees to help her search the hotel for Walter. Eve was overcome with worry. When they couldn't find him in the hotel, they started a search around the property. When they didn't find him there, they started a wider search. Eve went back to the hotel to ask anyone if they had seen him. She immediately ran into Annabelle and Millicent.

"I can't find my dad. I don't know where he is," Annabelle said frantically. "I can't believe I lost him again. What is he going to do this time? I was in the shower, and he must have left. Have you seen him?"

"No, we already looked in the hotel and now we are looking outside," said Eve. "I came in here to ask if anyone had seen him."

Millicent was eyeing Eve suspiciously. "How did you know he was missing?" she asked.

Eve explained how she had knocked on the door and it opened revealing that Walter wasn't in his room.

Annabelle shot her a guilty look before she said, "I need to go look for him." She hurried out the back door before Eve could say anything else.

"I'll go drive out to the cabins," offered Millicent. "Maybe he wanted to go home to his old cabin."

"That's a good idea, thanks." Eve stood motionless as she watched Millicent walk out of the front door. She was trying to determine the best course of action. Call search and rescue? Find out where the others were? Yes, she would enlist the help of everyone here first.

She knocked on Julie and Tom's door first. They answered and quickly joined the search party when they heard what happened. She knocked on Ben's door but there was no answer. She knocked on Gil's door but there was no answer. Then Sterling's, and again no answer. Perhaps one of them was with Walter and there was nothing to worry about. Or perhaps one of them was with Walter and there was something to worry about. Eve's mind was racing with any number of possibilities.

She decided to search the hotel again. Maybe they had missed something. She started in the basement, nothing. By the time she had finished searching the ground floor, she had made a decision. She went to the reservation desk and opened the small safe that housed the room keys. She grabbed the master key. As she headed up the stairs to search every room upstairs, occupied or not, she heard the front door open. She turned around so hopeful to see Walter that when she did see Walter, she didn't believe her eyes. She thought she must be hallucinating. But it was indeed Walter, safe and sound, accompanied by Millicent.

"I found him," she announced. "I called Annabelle and told her."

"Where was he?"

"Sitting on the front porch of his old cabin."

"You're a genius, Millicent."

"I know."

The back door swung open and Annabelle ran into the lobby towards her father.

He looked at her and said, "I'm tired."

"Okay, Dad. Let's go rest. I think we all need to rest now."

Annabelle took Walter back up to his suite. Eve clutched her chest and said to Millicent, "Yes, I believe it is customary to rest after having a heart attack."

Millicent appeared unruffled. "He was fine. There was no need to worry. What did y'all think was going to happen?" she asked rhetorically as she went to the dining room to get some breakfast.

Eve called her search party one by one to let them know that the search was over, and all was well. Eve prided herself on the calm collected way she delivered the information during each call. After she finished, she walked into her suite, threw herself on her bed and screamed into her pillow.

Chapter Thirty-Two

Eve stayed in her suite for a few more minutes to calm her nerves. She was about to exit into the lobby when she changed her mind and turned around. She needed some more alone time. She decided to go sit on her suite's small porch and enjoy the morning shade of the western side of the building.

With her, she brought scribbled notes that she needed to transform into the questions for Hotel History Trivia, the game she had scheduled for today. Over the course of the last few days, Eve had been using everyone's stories and history interviews to compile a list of trivia questions to use for the game. Her plan was to divide her guests into two groups and see who remembered the most from their days here.

She thought back to last week when she had come up with her brilliant idea to have a trivia game. Oh, what a fantasy she had of the joyous time that would be had by all playing this game on their last day here. How fun it would be, she had told herself— after a few days of reminiscing, everyone would get together and see if they were paying attention to each other's stories... But, in reality, this weekend had not turned out like that. In her imagined perfect reunion, Wes had not been shot, Walter had not gone missing, there had not been a blackout, and certainly there had not been the introduction of a resident ghost or the revelation of a decades old murder.

A sound made Eve look up from her notes. Because of her desire to be alone, the approaching footsteps through the nearby parking area caused her to uncharacteristically act like a possum. She immediately froze, hoping that her presence in the dark shade of the bright morning would go unnoticed by whomever was walking by.

Her intention was not to eavesdrop once again, but alas... This time, it was a conversation between Tom and Julie as they were making their way back to the hotel after searching for Walter. They were on the other side of the hedges that separated the parking lot from the hotel, but Eve easily recognized their voices.

"Everything's fine. At least they found him," said Julie.

"I know but maybe..." Tom trailed off.

"What? Maybe what?"

"We shouldn't have come here," said Tom.

"Maybe you and Ben shouldn't have come here," replied Julie crossly. "I like it here."

"I like it here too," Tom said. "You know I do. It's where I met you,"

The sound of footsteps stopped as Tom and Julie paused their progress. They had come to the break in the hedges where the path led to the hotel. Apparently, they stopped to finish their private conversation before arriving back to the building full of people. Little did they know that they had perfectly placed themselves in Eve's view.

"Oh, you regret marrying me," Julie said.

"No, I don't. What a stupid thing to say."

"Oh, I'm stupid now?"

"Be serious. Don't you know what I would do for

you?" Tom said with feeling. "What I did for you?"

"Maybe you did too much. I didn't ask you to do anything."

"Well, I did what I did, and you did what you did. There's no going back now."

The couple stared at each other in silence.

"What are you talking about?" Julie finally asked. "What did I do?"

"You want me to say it?"

"Yes, say it."

"Fine. I heard you that day, the day Dirk died. I heard you saying you were going out to the shooting range to practice because you wanted to get better at defending yourself. And you must have had to defend yourself sooner than you thought. You killed Dirk."

Silence followed by more silence. Eve had stopped breathing, for how long she didn't know. She thought she might pass out. She didn't know if she should say something. What would she say?

Julie was silently crying and shaking her head.

Eve felt horrible spying on this scene and decided she would alert them to her presence. Before she could determine the best way to go about doing it, she saw something out of the corner of her eye which caused her to gasp loudly.

It was Sterling. He was on the path to the parking lot. His natural stealth had prevented anyone from realizing his presence. But now that Eve had made her clumsy noise of surprise, Tom and Julie were aware that they had an audience. To Eve's surprise, Tom and Julie ignored both her presence and Sterling's. The married couple returned their concentration back to each other and continued their conversation.

When Julie finally managed to stop crying enough to speak, she looked at Tom and said, "I thought maybe you did it."

Tom's eyes teared up as he furrowed his brow and

shook his head. "No, I didn't do it," he said quietly.

"So, you always knew about me and Dirk?" Julie asked.

"Of course. You think that scumbag kept that to himself? He bragged to all the guys about how he used you. He was so proud of himself. He was trash through and through."

"I hoped you didn't know. I kept telling myself that you didn't. I was worried that if you knew, that might have meant you were the one who killed him."

"I didn't," Tom said soberly.

"But Dirk was covered in bruises," said Julie, "and you had that black eye. I thought you beat him up, so I thought it was a possibility that later you decided that wasn't enough, and you shot him."

Tom continued to shake his head. "No, I didn't beat him up. I was so angry with him for treating you badly. I hated him and I wanted him gone. I tried to talk to him, to get him to leave. But his response was to use me as a punching bag. I didn't know how to fight. Luckily, Leslie came to my rescue."

"Leslie? Who's Leslie?" Julie asked.

"Sterling. Leslie is his first name," Tom explained.

"Sterling beat him up?" asked a confused Julie. "Dirk was black and blue."

"He didn't mean to hurt him," said Tom, "At least not that bad."

Julie looked to Sterling for answers.

"It was his own fault," said Sterling. "He kept coming at me or going after Tom. He was like a rabid animal."

"It's true," agreed Tom. "There was no stopping him except by force."

"And by then, I had reason to hate Dirk," Sterling admitted. "He had borrowed money from me that he never intended on paying back, but I could overlook that. What I couldn't abide was his taking advantage of Daisy. Daisy didn't know any better. She was so innocent, so childlike. The more I thought about what a disgraceful sexual predator he was, the more I didn't mind punching him. I didn't even know that Tom was there trying to defend your honor. Only afterwards did Tom tell me, and I learned that Dirk was even worse than I thought.

"Of course, Tom and I never told anyone about the fight," Sterling continued. "After Dirk was shot, we were so worried that his death would get connected to us. One or both of us could have easily been arrested for his murder based on that fight. Tom had a black eye and I had bruised knuckles. If it had been anyone other than old Sheriff Weed, it could have turned out really bad for us. We told everyone that Tom got the black eye from getting bucked off a horse and vowed to say nothing else. We had every reason to want Dirk's death to be forgotten as soon as possible."

Up until this point, even though the three of them knew Eve was there, no one had acknowledged her presence. But at this moment, Tom looked directly at Eve and said, "I was scared that his death would get pinned on me, but I was even more scared that Julie would get arrested."

Julie placed one of her hands in Tom's as she wiped a tear from his face with the other.

Tom looked lovingly at his wife. "I really thought you did it," he mumbled. "I figured it was self-defense, but I thought you did it."

"I didn't," she said.

Eve looked at the couple. She wanted to believe the truthfulness of their statements and the emotional, romantic reunion. She had to admit, this story certainly explained some previous inconsistencies, most notably, Tom's black eye. During his interview he had told Eve that the black eye had been due to getting bucked off a horse, but she knew that to be a lie. During Storytime, he had said that the first and last time he had ever been bucked off a horse was on his second day of work.

Tom and Julie seemed sincere, but perhaps they were putting on a show for Eve's benefit. After all, everyone had been lying to her this weekend and Tom and Julie may be the most adept liars here. They had both worked as dealers in Vegas for years which meant they were trained to have good poker faces. And they had both been in the entertainment industry as well. Perhaps they both knew how to put on a good show.

And even if this scene was completely sincere and both of them didn't have anything to do with Dirk's death— at the time of Wes's shooting, which may have been intended for Gil— each thought the other was Dirk's murderer. One of them could have been attempting to protect the other.

Chapter Thirty-Three

Eve had moved into her office to try and buckle down to finish the trivia game questions for today. She thought moving to a more business-like atmosphere would help her work, but she was still having a hard time not thinking about the new information she had just learned. Her thoughts had become fixated on Sterling's comments when there was a soft knock on the office door.

"Come in," she called.

Daisy peeked her head in. "Do you want to do our history interview now? Millicent thought we could do ours together to save you some time."

"Sure," Eve replied distractedly.

Daisy and Millicent sat in the guest chairs on the opposite side of the desk. Eve's head was full of competing thoughts as she set up the audio recording app. She hit the play button but couldn't think of what to say. She turned off the recording and stared at the two women.

"Um... I don't know how to say this tactfully so I'm just going to ask."

"Isn't that what you're supposed to be doing? Asking

us questions?" Millicent asked in her usual snarky way.

"Is Christopher Daisy's son?" Eve asked Millicent.

Millicent shot her the patented Battleax Buchanan stare of disapproval. "That's not one of the questions you were supposed to ask," Millicent replied.

Daisy remained wide-eyed and silent.

"My great aunt had seen Daisy throwing up by the side of the building a few days before Annabelle left for boarding school which was shortly after Dirk's death," Eve explained. "She had been worried Daisy had the flu, but she obviously didn't because Daisy was at the goodbye gathering for Annabelle two days later. Then, Daisy stopped working at the hotel shortly afterwards. Daisy, you said you had left due to a family emergency, but I think Millicent probably taught you to say that in lieu of 'in a family way' and you simply had morning sickness when Genevieve saw you.

"And you told me that you went to live with family in What Cheer," Eve said to Daisy. "I happen to know that town is in Iowa." She then focused her gaze on Millicent. "And a few days ago, Millicent, you mentioned your sister in Iowa knew of a baby that needed a home. You also said that you adopted Christopher in the spring of the following year that Daisy left. And Sterling just alerted me to the fact that Dirk had taken advantage of Daisy's trusting nature in more than one way."

Daisy looked at Millicent for direction. Millicent nodded to her and addressed Eve.

"Yes. It's true. It's not a secret. Not really, not anymore. Christopher knows that Daisy is his biological mother. Buck never knew, but after he passed, I told Christopher that Daisy was his mom. She would come visit every once in a while when he was growing up, so he already knew her." Millicent took a deep breath. "Daisy was so ashamed when she found out she was pregnant. She didn't want anyone at the hotel to find out. So, she went to go live with family. It was just my family, not hers."

"I was so happy Millicent could take the baby," said Daisy. "I couldn't have taken care of him. He had such a wonderful childhood with Buck and Millicent," she said sweetly before her face suddenly darkened. "But we don't want Christopher to know who his father was," said Daisy nervously.

"Your secret is safe with me," Eve assured them.

"Luckily, the only thing Christopher inherited from Dirk was his looks," said Millicent. "Daisy and I decided long ago to keep our secret. Even when we told him about Daisy being his mother, we just told him that his biological father was a cowboy that breezed in and out of town before anyone knew his last name. That seemed to be enough of an explanation for him. No good would come from him knowing that his biological father was a scoundrel."

"A murdered scoundrel," Eve clarified. "But yes, I am in complete agreement, and as I already said, your secret is safe with me."

"Thank you," said Millicent. "Because if anyone here finds out that Daisy is Christopher's mother, they might put two and two together and figure out that Dirk is Christopher's…" She trailed off and shook her head. "I hate even saying it out loud."

"And then if they know, Christopher might find out somehow," Daisy said, completing Millicent's thought. "So, no one here can know."

"But Sterling might know already," suggested Eve.

"He might?" Millicent asked.

"Yes," Eve replied. "He knew that Dirk had taken advantage of Daisy. He also witnessed her getting sick that day and took her home at the bequest of my great aunt. And he…" Eve stopped herself. She didn't know whether she should reveal the rest of her knowledge.

"He beat up Dirk," Daisy completed the sentence.

"Yes," said Eve. "How did you know?"

"I saw. I snuck away and followed him."

"She was always sneaking off and following boys," Millicent clucked disapprovingly. "I always wondered who beat up Dirk before he died. It was Sterling?"

Eve relayed the story that she had just been told.

"I never guessed it was him," Millicent said. "Honestly, I thought it was Buck."

Eve wanted to hear the rest of Daisy's story. "So, Daisy, you followed Sterling…" she prompted.

"Sterling was so kind to me," Daisy said dreamily. "I liked him. I just wanted to talk to him some more that day, so I followed him. But when he found Dirk hitting Tom, I hid behind a tree. But I could still see a little. Sterling was so mad. I heard him saying something about me. Dirk was so scary. It was then that I realized how truly wicked he was."

"And that's why you thought Ernest killed him?"

Daisy cowered under the glowering gaze of Millicent. After a moment, she said, "That's why I think he was killed."

"But you don't actually think it was Ernest? Or some other ghost?"

Daisy remained quiet.

Eve was getting desperate to solve this mystery. "I told you that I wouldn't tell anyone about Christopher. Do you believe that I will keep my word?"

"Yes," replied Daisy.

"Then, I will make a second promise to you. Whatever you tell me right now, will not leave this room," Eve said.

Millicent started to look worried but said nothing.

"Did you follow someone? Did you see someone kill Dirk?" Eve asked Daisy.

"No, nothing like that," said Daisy.

"Please, Daisy," Eve pleaded.

"Go ahead Daisy," said Millicent.

With Millicent's approval Daisy took a deep breath and said, "After the fight, Sterling found me behind the tree and realized I had seen the whole thing. He made me promise to not tell anyone about the fight."

"That's all?" Eve asked.

"He also told me not to worry about Dirk anymore," Daisy said slowly. "He told me that he would make sure Dirk never hurt me again. He would make sure Dirk never even talked to me again."

"And you assumed Sterling killed Dirk?" Eve asked.

"I was worried it was Sterling. And if it was Sterling, then it was my fault— MY fault. I told myself it was Ernest and I told everyone else it was Ernest. It really made the most sense to me. It had to be him. Nobody knew what happened, it was all so mysterious, it seemed most likely. And I really wanted everyone to believe that it was a ghost and not a person because I didn't want Sterling to get in trouble for protecting me. I convinced myself that Ernest killed Dirk to punish him for his wickedness."

Eve was disappointed. She thought perhaps Daisy had held the answer to her question. But it still loomed. Perhaps it would be best if Eve also convinced herself that Ernest killed Dirk so she could move on with her life! Maybe it isn't ignorance that is bliss, maybe it's 'full-blown delusion is bliss.'

Eventually the history interview began, and Eve found out a lot more information about the hotel that was a lot less dramatic, but more useful for her project. And most importantly, Millicent gave her the prized meatloaf recipe.

After the two ladies left, Eve thought about the secret that they had shared for a lifetime and how protecting a baby from his wicked father would be a fierce motive for murder.

But they all had motives. Dirk was a truly horrible person whom everyone hated. Eve wondered why she cared who murdered him. But, of course, she knew why: Wes. Instilled in her was fierce desire to protect the work family she had assembled. She could not overlook the shooting of one of her employees. She was now completely confident that the two shootings were connected and could think of nothing else. Perhaps no one else believed her but she hadn't been able to shake the feeling. She needed to rely on her intuition and she wanted to unearth the truth. She needed to.

Chapter Thirty-Four

It was time for Hotel History Trivia. Eve sadly remembered the time when she had been so excited for this event. Ramon and all her guests were present except for Walter who was napping and Ben who had no interest and stayed in his room. As she looked at the two groups she had divided on the couches and chairs in the lobby she realized she couldn't focus on her game. She was overwhelmed with thoughts of Wes's shooting and Dirk's shooting, 46 years earlier.

The more she thought about it, the more she believed that Gil was the key to the mystery. Gil was the one playing tricks by keeping things from her. She had determined that was what her magician dream had been trying to tell her. Perhaps if she could get Gil to come clean… if her suspicions were correct, if she could pull that first thread, then maybe she could get the rest of the truth to unravel.

She looked at the group and announced, "I have a list of trivia questions here, but I don't care about the answers to these questions right now. I only have two questions for you all: Who shot Wes? And Who shot Dirk?"

She looked at each of the uncomfortable faces before she rested her gaze on her target.

"Gil, I thought someone had tried to kill you, but you obviously did not agree. But someone did shoot at you and Wes. So, why would you protect someone who shot at you? That never made any sense. I feared for your life, but you didn't. You kept trying to tell me it was an accident. How could it be an accident? I decided that the only way that you could have been sure it was an accident was if you had seen the person who took the shot. I decided that you must have seen Ben. Ben was the one who was talking about wanting to go shooting. I decided that you had witnessed Ben irresponsibly messing around with your gun and when the shot was fired you could tell it was a mistake, an accident. Ben reminds you of your son, so you felt the natural inclination to protect him. That made sense to me.

"But last night before dinner," she continued. "I found out that was not what happened. Ben had told me he was in his room all morning but no one saw him. But it turned out that he did have an alibi, someone did see him. So, it wasn't Ben. If it wasn't Ben, who else would you see shoot at you and yet feel the need to protect?

"I visualized every person shooting at you and only one explanation made sense. There is only one person here who you would feel the need to protect, who you hold in high regard that you wouldn't hold accountable for his actions: Walter— Mr. Flint."

Gil quickly looked at Annabelle before turning back to Eve. He nodded his head sadly. "Well… yes. I saw him, Wes didn't. After he shot the gun once, he jumped back and ran off. He was confused, he didn't mean to do it. I called Annabelle, not 911 like you thought I did."

"I had been looking for my dad," said Annabelle. "He had wandered off and I was getting worried. When Gil called and told me what happened, it was like my worst nightmare was coming true. So, I hurried out to try and find him."

"I thought you were inappropriately dressed for a hike," Eve said to Annabelle. "And you always wear the perfect outfit for every occasion."

Annabelle let out a little laugh despite the seriousness of the situation.

"I wanted you to take Wes to the hospital," Gil said to Eve, "so that I could go find Mr. Flint and get the gun from him. But I couldn't come up with a good explanation to do that after you suggested someone was shooting at me."

"So, I went and found my dad," said Annabelle.

"Did you take a horse out? You had horsehair on your pants, and they weren't the same pants you wore the day before, as you had suggested."

"I took her," said Sterling.

Eve gave him a look of exasperation. *Was everyone in on this secret?* She looked at him for more information.

"I did hear the gun shot," Sterling admitted. "I was concerned, so I rode out to where I thought it came from. I came across Annabelle, and she told me what happened. I gave her a ride so we could find Mr. Flint as soon as possible. When we found him, I took the rifle and put it in my bag. By the time I rode back, put away my horse, and brushed her down, Mr. Flint and Annabelle were just making their way back to the hotel on foot."

"I really thought you had the rifle in your duffel bag," said Eve. "Or that maybe you carried your own rifle around in there."

"I know you did," said Sterling. "That's why I made a big show out of opening my bag in front of you later to show you that I carried a tripod, not a gun."

"And did you station yourself near the shooting range for your bird watching to cover up any of Walter's footprints?"

"It occurred to me that Mr. Flint may have dropped something or left some sort of incriminating evidence out there, so I went out to check. I stomped around the area just in case."

She continued to stare at Sterling. "And you were the one who left the rifle on the bar in such a dramatic fashion last night during the blackout?"

"Yes," he replied with a hint of embarrassment. "But in my defense, that was not my intention. I told Gil I would take care of the gun. My plan was simply to place it back onto Gil's gun rack when no one was around. I was headed outside to do it when your young employee corralled me into the dining room. Once the lights went out and the storm was about to hit, I knew there was no way I was going to be able to casually stroll out to the parking lot unnoticed. So, I took advantage of the situation and got the gun out of my possession by laying it on the bar."

Eve looked at Annabelle, Gil, and Sterling. "If you all thought Walter was just confused and it was an accident, why didn't you all just tell me the truth?"

"Well, I think at first, we could only think of protecting Mr. Flint," said Gil. But, after the dust settled, we probably would have told you, but then you called in the sheriff. At that point, the three of us decided to keep quiet to make sure Mr. Flint didn't get arrested."

Eve took turns looking at Annabelle, Gil, and Sterling. "Is that why? Is that really why? Or is it because you suspected that Walter was actually trying to shoot Gil to cover up the murder of Dirk?"

"Mr. Flint? You think he killed Dirk and was trying to silence me? No way," scoffed Gil.

"Maybe. Or maybe he was trying to protect the person that did kill Dirk. You all talked about how he was willing to help you all out when you were in need."

"What are you suggesting?" asked Tom.

"At first, I was horrified at how you all seemed to disregard Dirk's murder," said Eve. "But the more I learned about Dirk, the more I understood. I started to get an understanding of Dirk's personality. And I must say, he must have been a truly disturbed person. He obviously took great pleasure from taking advantage of any situation and any person that he could. In particular, he liked manipulating weak women. He shared many behavior characteristics of misogynistic men that become serial killers. I don't often use the word evil to describe someone, but in this case I believe the word fits Dirk.

"Sterling mentioned that Dirk had taken advantage of Daisy's childlike innocence. He used the words 'sexual predator' to describe Dirk. Sterling was right, Dirk was a predator. Julie finally admitted to me that she not only knew Dirk but that she had a brief relationship with him, a very disagreeable one. When he tossed her aside, he told her that she was too old for him and yet at only 20 years old, Julie was the youngest lady working at the hotel."

"What does that mean?" asked Tom defensively.

"It means that there was only one female at the ranch that was younger than that, the 13-year-old daughter of the hotel manager and his wife. The 13-year-old girl who had won multiple sharp shooting trophies. The girl who was abruptly sent off to boarding school right after Dirk's murder. Who would Walter feel the need to protect more than his own daughter?"

Annabelle erupted into a fit of sobbing.

"No!" shouted Millicent as she walked over to Annabelle and put her arm around her violently shaking shoulders. "No," she said more calmly. "Annabelle was with me that entire day. Constance and I took Annabelle to town with us to do some shopping before Mr. Thorton's arrival. She wasn't here. I swear. She wasn't here."

Eve was sure Millicent would say or do anything to protect Annabelle. Eve looked at the sobbing Annabelle and suddenly felt horrible for her. No matter the outcome of this conversation, it was not one to be had in front of an audience. She asked Millicent and Annabelle to join her in her office.

After the majority of hysteria subsided, Eve said, "I'm sorry Annabelle. I truly am. But you need to tell me what happened. Did Dirk hurt you?"

Annabelle shook her head but wouldn't or couldn't speak yet.

While Millicent held Annabelle's hand, Eve patiently waited for her to collect herself. As she did, she started to think about Annabelle's behavior over the course of the last few days. If she had killed Dirk as a child, accidentally or not, why would she come back here to relive bad memories? She seemed genuinely happy to be here at first. After the shooting, Annabelle started acting a little stressed and guarded but she was still good company when she knew her father was safely in his room. That made sense given what Eve had just learned. But in the last day she started acting like she was going to have a nervous breakdown and was hiding away her father as much as she could. And she had been packed and ready to leave this morning.

"Annabelle, did something happen yesterday?" Eve asked. "Did your dad say something? Did you find out something?"

Annabelle nodded. Eve waited.

"I was always so happy here," said Annabelle finally. "I didn't know why my parents suddenly sent me off to boarding school, but I guess it was to protect me. Maybe to protect me from the harm they perceived might be here or to protect me from finding out the truth." She choked back a sob. "I thought bringing my dad here would be good for him. But it has brought back the bad memories along with the good ones." She looked into Millicent's eyes and squeezed her hand. "Buck didn't kill Dirk, Millie. Dad did."

Now it was Millicent's turn to start crying.

Annabelle waited for Millicent to wipe her last tear away before she began her story. "My dad started talking about something yesterday, I wasn't even really paying attention until I realized this was the most he had spoken since his arrival here. He wasn't even talking to me, I'm not sure who he thought he was talking to. I was horrified when I realized he was talking about shooting Dirk. I thought he must be confused, so I started asking him questions to clarify. But what I found out shocked me.

"I have only a convoluted idea of the conversation that my father had with Dirk. Dad was target shooting alone when Dirk appeared and decided to rile him up, I guess. Dirk said some horrible things about liking little girls, and that he had his eye on me. From what I gathered, Dad killed him in a moment of blind rage. But then he made a comment to me— or to someone else, or the world in general— that he didn't regret killing Dirk. He said that if he just fired Dirk, he probably would have just gone somewhere else and found another young girl to accost. He said he couldn't have him arrested for something he hadn't done yet and he wasn't about to wait until Dirk put his dirty hands on his daughter or anyone's daughter before he was punished. He was glad he did the world a favor and got rid of him first. He said Dirk wasn't a man, he was vermin and needed to be killed and disposed of, that he was just trash that needed to be taken out.

"I gathered that he radioed the sheriff, and they had Dirk's body removed before anyone knew what happened. I don't know if he told Sheriff Weed the truth, or if he told Buck, or my mom. Perhaps yesterday was the first time he ever said it out loud.

"I've been hiding him away ever since. I've been so scared he would tell that story again to someone else. That's why I was going to try and sneak him out of here this morning. And maybe I would have got away with it if I hadn't taken that stupid shower. And if I hadn't brought ten suitcases I had to try to smuggle out of here!" Annabelle started laughing a tad wildly before she suddenly stopped and very sadly said, "What am I going to do?"

"I don't know," said Eve kindly, "but your dad has reached a point where he can be dangerous. Wes's getting shot may have been an accident, but we can't rule out the possibility that he was trying to silence Gil and keep his involvement in Dirk's murder a secret."

"No, I can't believe for one minute that my father, in any state of mind, would attempt to kill an innocent man to protect himself. Never." Annabelle looked at Eve defiantly.

"I agree," said Millicent.

They all stared at each other, none of them knowing what to say next. A knock on the door made all three ladies jump.

"Come in," Eve called.

The door opened. It was Sterling. "Annabelle, your dad just woke up and came down."

They all exited the office and joined the others in the lobby with Walter. Everyone was awkwardly quiet. At that moment, Wes walked into the lobby from the dining room.

"Hey," he said cautiously, obviously sensing the unease in the room. "I just wanted to know if —" Wes stopped talking when he saw Walter charging at him like a bull.

Walter's arms were stretched out, his hands positioned to choke the life out of Wes. "Why aren't you dead?" Walter cried. "I shoot you and shoot you, Dirk, but you won't die! You need to die!"

Chapter Thirty-Five

The Grand Opening was a grand success if Eve said so herself, which she did at that very moment to Ramon.

"Agreed," said Ramon. "Except that it is a travesty that I have not won a single cake walk."

"I'm sure that Esperanza will make you the cake of your desire after this is over. After all, you won the best prize of all: being married to the baker." Eve smiled as she looked over the crowd of people having fun swimming, eating, riding horses, playing games and socializing.

"True. Has anyone won the celebrated cow plop yet?" Ramon asked.

Eve had been delighted to incorporate the fun ranch tradition at the last minute. Wes's girlfriend, June, borrowed a cow from her ranch for the honor. And, as planned, she had also taken the day off to come help Wes with the free horseback rides.

"I heard a rumor that Dr. Nadar won the cow plop," said Eve. "There was some scuttlebutt that as a veterinarian, she must have had some secret way of securing her win."

Eve scanned the crowd for Naiya's distinctive black

bob. She spotted her holding the very noticeable oversized plush cow with the Dancer Diner gift certificate attached to it. Eve walked over to her.

"So, it's true," Eve said. "You do have a way to telepathically communicate with animals."

"Just to tell them to defecate on command," Naiya replied. "It usually doesn't come in very handy, but today all those years of training paid off," she said as she ceremoniously held the soft, giant cow toy over her head.

As she held up her trophy, both Naiya and Eve noticed a little girl looking up longingly at the stuffed animal. Naiya untied the gift certificate and presented the cow to the girl. The cow was nearly as big as she was, but her pride in her new toy gave her the determination and strength to run away with it as fast as she could to show her mom and dad.

"I'm keeping this!" Naiya said as she put the gift certificate in her purse. "Oh, and I love your mom."

"Yes, everybody does. It's hard not to love the lady who brought a hot air balloon to the party."

Minna had showed up the day before with a man and his hot air balloon. He had been giving people tethered hot air balloon rides all day. Eve had to admit, it made the event ten times more fun and memorable. Her mom always had that effect. She always made everything more fun or more memorable and most of the time, both.

"I should probably get going," said Naiya. "Is Midas still in your suite?"

"Yes, I just checked on them. Both Sunset and Midas were still snoozing away. They played hard and now they're sleeping hard. Midas was even snoring!"

"Oh yes, slobbering and snoring, that's the guy I sleep with. Oh, my glamorous life."

When they went into her suite to wake up Midas and Sunset, Eve said, "For your information... I know Gil took Wes out to see you instead of taking him to the hospital."

"He told you?" she asked cautiously.

"No. I figured it out partly because Gil came back with the Midas touch," she said as she cupped Midas's adorable, slobbery face.

"I swear, this dog will be the end of me," Naiya joked before she became serious. "Gil is a good guy and I owed him a favor. A few months ago, I was at Dancer Diner and I got an emergency call, a horse was having complications birthing her foal. I was in a panic to get out to the ranch, but my car wouldn't start. Gil drove me out there and stayed with me for hours acting as my assistant. Then he drove me back to my car. During the time we were gone, he had his mechanic come and fix my car. I told him I owed him one, a big one, and I meant it. So, when he came to collect that favor, I couldn't say no. Plus, I trust Gil, I really do. So, even though I thought Wes's injury may have been a bullet wound, I trusted that nothing nefarious was at play. Accidents happen. I figured he must have a good reason for coming to me and I didn't ask. But I did ask him and Wes to swear to not tell anyone about my involvement. I could get in a lot of trouble if I was to be found administering medical care to humans. I hope you understand."

Eve told her that she understood and said she would keep it under her hat.

"Are you still game on going into the wine business together?" Eve asked.

"Yes! I'm glad you brought it up. I was thinking that we could call it Naïve Wines but spell it N-a-i-E-v-e!"

"Sure, your name goes first I see," Eve teased.

"Oh, I didn't really think—"

"I'm kidding! I love it! NaiEve, it's our names together and we are naïve about making wine!"

"Exactly!"

Naiya and Eve made plans to get together soon. Then Sunset and Eve said goodbye to their new friends, Midas and Naiya.

Eve took Sunset out to the party. She knew he was

tired enough that he would behave himself and not jump on any of the remaining children. As soon as Sunset spotted Tom and Julie, his tail started wagging double-time.

"There you are, Sunset!" Tom bent down and started scratching Sunset's ears.

Tom, Julie and Ben had stayed on after the others had left and had become Eve's first paying hotel guests. Tom and Julie had spent the last few days looking for property in the area. Yesterday, they had put in an offer on a small house with a few acres about 10 miles from the hotel. It was amazing to see the transformation in their marriage. The decades of suspecting each other of murder had taken its toll. But now, they seemed free and happy to be starting a new chapter in their lives. Ben, on the other hand was unhappy to find that his new chapter involved having to move out of the house in Las Vegas that his parents were going to sell.

"I saw your impromptu magic show with the kids earlier," Eve said to Tom.

"My magic skills are pretty rusty, but I still have the ability to impress very young children," he laughed.

"Well then, I must be a very young child because I was impressed," said Eve. "You know, when the rifle appeared on the bar during the blackout, my first thought was that it seemed like a magic trick and you must have been the one behind it because of your background."

"I must admit, I considered that also," said Julie. "I still thought that Ben might have been the one who accidentally shot Wes, and Tom was covering for him."

"Yes," said Tom with a smile. "But that was way back, last week, when we weren't being completely open and honest with each other like we are now."

"I must admit," said Julie, "I feel much more at ease knowing my husband didn't shoot Dirk, and my son didn't shoot Wes. Much, much more at ease."

The couple smiled at each other.

"Good, I'm glad. I also saw that you two were helping Wes and June with the horse rides today," said Eve. "Thank you so much. I really appreciate that. I obviously needed even more help than I realized. But now I feel bad that I let you pay for your rooms for the last few days."

"We insisted, remember?" said Julie. "And we are happy to help. We love your horses. I hope we can afford to get a couple ourselves."

"Thanks again for the reunion," said Tom. "I know it didn't exactly go according to plan, but it has changed our lives for the better. I hope to stay in touch with Leslie too."

"That reminds me," Eve said. "I was confused by one of my Great Aunt Genevieve's letters that mentioned a Leslie and a Fergus. Now I know who Leslie is, but I still don't know Fergus. Any chance that either of you knew a Fergus working here at the hotel or the ranch?"

"Fergus? No, I don't think— wait," said Tom. "I think maybe Fergus was Buck's real name. I think Buck was actually a nickname for Buchanan."

"That makes sense," said Eve. "Also, I've been meaning to ask you guys about Sterling. Did I hear something about him and Daisy leaving together?"

Julie laughed. "As they were all getting ready to go, Daisy admitted to Sterling that she had always been madly in love with… birdwatching." Julie laughed again. "So, he invited her to join him on his excursion to Lake Mead."

"Hey," Eve said as she joined Julie in the amusement of the situation, "if she can genuinely take an interest in birdwatching, it might just work!"

"Oh, Eve," said Julie, "By the way, I wanted to tell you that your mom is fabulous!"

At that moment, Sheriff Strider walked up to the three of them. Julie took her husband's arm and gently pulled him to start walking away as Julie gave Eve the slightest of winks.

"Nobody ever calls me fabulous," Eve muttered to

herself. When she saw that Sunset was following Tom and Julie she called out, "Traitor!" to the back side of her dog.

"It's hard to find good loyal companions these days," said Strider. "So, today was a hit. Good job."

"I know Roxie's happy about it." She nodded her head over to where Roxie was talking with Deputy Navarro, her current crush.

"When I suggested we come out, he seemed very interested."

Gil walked up to the two of them. "I'm sorry to interrupt," he said. "I just wanted to apologize again to you Eve, and apologize to you, Sheriff. I was so sure that Mr. Flint shot Wes by accident, but I was wrong. I'm sorry. If I would have known that he did it on purpose... well... if I would have known that his confusion was making him dangerous, I would have said something. I'm really sorry." And with that, he walked off. Gil had already profusely apologized to Eve but apparently, he needed to apologize to the law as well to clear his conscience. Gil Dancer really was a good guy. Eve would have to go to see him at Dancer Diner sometime.

Eve turned serious as she turned back to the sheriff. "Thanks for helping Annabelle with her dad."

When Walter had lunged at Wes, Tom and Sterling quickly grabbed Walter and subdued him. At that point, Eve had decided to call Sheriff Strider and tell him everything. He had been effective in taking care of a complicated situation that no one else had known how to handle.

"No problem. It's not the first time I've had to deal with something like that. This was more complex, but the solution was the same."

"Your friend down in Phoenix got him set up in a memory care facility?"

"Yes. It's near where Annabelle lives. It's a nice facility."

Eve wondered if she should even bring this up, but she couldn't help but asking, "And what about Dirk's murder?"

"I'm not going to reopen a closed 46-year-old accidental death case with no physical evidence based on the possible confession of a man in a memory care facility. That would be a waste of taxpayers' money."

"Isn't spending your time coming out to a grand opening party a waste of taxpayers' money?" she said teasingly.

"Are you kidding? Since your property seems to be a hotbed of mystery and intrigue, I believe it a necessary duty to come out here on a regular basis to check up on you."

Ben walked up wearing a T-shirt that said, "Bigfoot saw me but nobody believes him." Ben, unlike Gil, completely ignored the fact that Eve was already having a conversation with someone else. "Hey, Eve. Since my parents told me I have to move out and get a job... Can I work here? You have those cabins out there. I could be like your IT guy or something."

Eve stammered only slightly before telling Ben that they were not hiring at the moment. Then, suddenly, she had an idea and excused herself. When she returned a few minutes later, Strider was awkwardly fielding questions about the guns used in the sheriff's department.

"Ben, I need to talk to the sheriff alone," Eve said decisively.

Ben left. Strider looked concerned.

"What is it?" he asked in a worried tone.

"Nothing, I was just coming to your aid for once," she said with a mischievous smile. "But I did want to tell you that you were right."

"About what? I mean, don't get me wrong, I love being told I'm right. Feel free to do it anytime, even if you don't have a reason."

"About your presence encouraging people to lie. If I

hadn't called you in after Wes got shot, I probably would have been able to get to the truth much faster. But since I had a sheriff with me, everyone got scared and defensive, and saw me as a possible threat because I was associated with the big bad law."

"It often happens. People have some secret or suspicion that scares them into silence, or worse, they try to direct blame at someone else to get themselves out of the spotlight."

"And that is exactly what happened. Millicent was defensive because she was so afraid that it would come to light that her husband was a murderer. Not only were Julie and Tom afraid the other had killed Dirk, but they were also both worried that their son accidentally shot Wes. Gil, Sterling, and Annabelle were all so worried that Walter's confusion would get him arrested. So, I guess, next time I won't call you."

"Hey now, let's not make any rash decisions. I could always come in my civilian clothes on my days off."

"You have days off? What's that like?"

"Maybe you need to hire some more people."

Eve positioned herself so that she was facing away from the crowd. She leaned in and whispered, "I just did. I hired Tom and Julie to take care of the horses on Wes's days off."

"Why are you whispering?" Strider whispered melodramatically.

"Because I don't want Ben to know that I hired his parents two minutes after I told him I wasn't hiring. Which, by the way, at the time I said it, was a true statement."

"And speaking of true statements, I must admit that you were right as well."

"About what?" Eve asked.

"You thought the same person was responsible for both Dirk's death and Wes's shooting," he explained.

"But I was wrong about why! It seems so obvious

now, that Walter would have mistaken Wes for Dirk while in a confused state of mind. They do look so much alike. At one point I thought perhaps Gil was mistaken for Tom, but it never occurred to me that Wes might have been mistaken for Dirk!" Eve again turned serious as she said, "I am so thankful that Walter's shooting skills were rusty. I can't even imagine if…" Eve felt herself getting emotional and shook it off. She forced a smile and said, "So, like I said, I was wrong about why Wes was shot!"

"But the two shootings were definitely connected. Your knee-jerk instinct was correct. You have an impressive intuition."

Eve childishly rolled her eyes at the compliment.

"We have a call," said a voice behind Eve that made her jump. It was Deputy Navarro, the young man that embodied the phrase "tall, dark, and handsome." She understood Roxie's attraction to him but doubted the two would be a successful match. Roxie was such a naturally silly girl and even though only a few years older than Roxie, Deputy Navarro was so very serious. But who knew, opposites often attract. Perhaps she would be the yin to his yang.

Strider nodded to Navarro in recognition that they were leaving immediately. To Eve he said, "Congratulations again on the grand opening. Well done."

"Thank you."

Sheriff Strider walked a few steps before he turned around and said, "And by the way, you're fabulous." He quickly turned back and resumed his exit march.

Eve desperately wanted to hide her smile from her approaching mother but found it impossible to put it away. But Minna surprised her by not commenting on it.
***

That evening, when the party had been put away and the guests had left or retired to their rooms, Eve and Minna sat on the veranda. Their entertainment was watching a storm roll in and watching Sunset try to catch his confusingly intangible nemesis, the thunder.

"I want to go target shooting at your shooting range while I'm here," said Minna.

"Seriously, Mother?"

"Yes. Your grandfather taught me how to shoot when I was a teenager. I think it's time for a refresher course."

"I'm not going to reopen the shooting range."

"You don't have to open it back up for guests. You can just take advantage of it for personal use."

Eve shook her head.

"When in Rome…," continued Minna. "Loosen up, darling. You live in the Wild West now. You need to be, well, a little more… wild."

Eve looked at her mother, and as usual, gave in. "Maybe," she said. But they both knew that her 'maybe' was an 'alright.' Eve had learned a long time ago that she would eventually bend to her mother's will so she may as well do it sooner than later. She also knew that Minna's suggestions to experience things outside of her comfort zone almost always ended with beneficial results.

"Good! And to foster this new wild side of yours… First thing tomorrow morning," Minna announced, "we're going on a hot air balloon ride. A real one, not tethered."

"I don't know…" Eve said hesitantly.

"You don't have to know because I know. You are going to love seeing your new home from the air. Plus, honey, it's the kind of adventure women like us are supposed to have." Minna gave her daughter the mischievous smile that she had inherited from her as she said, "You know, because we're fabulous."